Dragon Tails

Meeting Diamond Beasties

GAIL KRAFT

Align Well Enterprises Publishing Division

Dragon Tails

Meeting Diamond Beasties

Published by Align Well Enterprises

eBook ISBN - 978-0-9891443-8-4

Paperback ISBN - 978-0-9891443-7-7

DISCLAIMER

The contents of this publication are intended for entertainment purposes and to peak the reader's curiosity. This is a work of fiction with the main characters based on Diana Cooper's amazing oracle cards, Dragon. Names, characters, businesses, places, events, locales, and incidents are either the products of the author's imagination or used in a fictitious manner. Any resemblance to an actual person or people, living or dead, or actual events is purely coincidental. The intent is both entertainment and enlightenment as to what could be. Please note, before digging deep into enlightenment and self-actualization it is important to obtain guidance from an authentic guide and to have support from a strong community.

The dragon's tail is covered in shimmering iridescent scales that reflect hues of blue, purple, and gold. It glows softly with a mystical aura, surrounded by sparkles and faint wisps of magical energy. The background is a dreamy twilight sky with stars and faint clouds, enhancing the fantasy atmosphere.

"I like nonsense, it wakes up the brain cells. Fantasy is a necessary ingredient in living."
~ Dr. Seuss

"The moment you doubt whether you can fly, you cease for ever to be able to do it."
~ J. M. Barrie, Peter Pan

"Dragons and legends...It would have been difficult for any man not to want to fight beside a dragon."
~ Patricia Briggs

"It's simply not an adventure worth telling if there aren't any dragons."
~ Sarah Ban Breathnach

"I fell in love with Dragon Tails. Its blend of child-like magic and deep wisdom reconnects us with our truth as Divine creators. I enjoyed witnessing the character's spiritual awakening and felt, viscerally, their transcendence into higher dimensions - an invitation for us to call dragons in to guide our own individual quest. The story opens up our imagination, provides us with a path to breaking through the limitations of three-dimensional thinking, and invites us into expanded states of consciousness, offering a fresh lens to see that our possibilities are truly limitless."

Tina Lyn Fiori, Soulenergee
Divine Alchemist

"Gail, Gail, Gail, your book is magnificent! It is a true inspiration. I absolutely loved it! I am so excited for you and for everyone who gets the opportunity to read and experience it."

Cindy Edington
Founder of Tranquil Heart Wellness

Forward

There are books you read... and then there are books that open something inside you. Dragon Tails – Meeting the Diamond Beasties, is an invitation back into imagination, not as escapism, but as a way to reconnect with guidance, healing, and possibility. In a world that often rewards logic and speed, Gail reminds us that wonder isn't childish, it's sacred. It's a doorway back to yourself.

What makes this book stand out is that the dragons aren't just fantasy characters. They arrive with purpose. Each encounter feels like a soulful mini-journey, carrying a specific lesson and energy: grounding with the Earth Dragon, balance through the Fire-and-Water Dragon, and clearing what no longer serves through the Fire Dragon and so much more as the pages unfold. Gail's writing is gentle and nurturing, yet clear. The imagery is vivid enough that you can see it, feel it, and soften into it.

And then Gail offers something rare: the experience continues beyond the page. At the end of the book you'll find a meditation for each dragon, with recordings accessed, so you don't just read about the dragons... you meet them. You are guided by Gail's own voice, and that matters. I personally experienced one of her meditations recently when she hosted our

MRS Potts Meeting in our *Diamond Beauties Forever* group, and I absolutely loved it. Her guidance is calm, heart-led, and beautifully grounding, the kind that helps your whole system exhale.

This book is for anyone who feels the pull to remember: your intuition, your inner world, your joy, your courage to believe again. Whether you're deeply spiritual or simply curious, Gail makes space for you here. Gail, your dragons are a gift. Your words are an opening. And your voice is a journey. Thank you for bringing the magic back.

With love and sunshine, Mwah!

Sanet Van Breda
CEO Your Voice TV Network
Founder of Diamond Beauties Forever

Contents

00 – Introduction – Where Has All the Magic Gone?

"Imagination will often carry us to worlds that never were. But without it we go nowhere." – Carl Sagan

You are invited to join me as I travel into a world of imagination that has been blended with a collection of dragon encounters. These are tales about the various dragons from the cosmos, a life many have stopped imagining existing. A place where possibilities lie beyond our dreams. An experience where something grand is always happening. I wonder:

- When did we become so logical that this third dimensional world became our everything?

- Where did our magic and imagination go?

- What is the judgment we hold onto that blocks our ability to dream?

- What is the fear that holds us back from proclaiming our joy in fanciful experiences?

Balance - magic presents possibilities and logic bring them into life.

As a child I was out of touch with living in this world, I was very much living in my mind, exploring with my imagination. I spent many hours alone as my older siblings worked or dated, then married and left. My mom completed her earthly role when I was three so was barely influential in my life and my dad worked evenings, thus not home with me after school.

Summers meant I had to be dealt with. I went away to relatives or camp, which made strong connections with neighborhood friends difficult to maintain. This alone time, this solo existence, gave me space to imagine and dream. In my world I believed I could feel things others could not. I knew that I could do things others could not. I could foresee things others did not. And it felt real, and it felt normal.

In my early teens my life was suddenly torn apart, and I was left to figure this world out without guidance or a roadmap.[1] This was a moment of abandonment that I could not bear. I put a wall up and made a decision to figure life out on my own. I went down the path of determination and the road of making harsh choices. I went down the road of logic.

As a young adult I made a living on analytical thinking, reasoning, and process. I was very successful being

---

[1] I go into detail about this experience in my chapter, *Left Behind, Again and Again* in the book *Women with Healing Gifts*

detail-oriented, rational, and organized. I “got things done.” I enjoyed life in this manner and had closed the door to a nagging feeling that I was missing something. I was always busy doing and creating and had become an expert at pretending everything was alright.

And then this life of “success” I built fell apart, like a house of cards, and I had to face me, the only real thing there actually is in this life, and I didn’t even know what that meant. I was lost, confused, and empty. I looked in the mirror and knew the answers were there. They had always been within me.

I started exploring and asking questions. In this quest of looking beyond logic I tapped into creativity, imagination, holistic thinking, intuition, and life’s rhythm. I began making choices based on my feelings and once again daydreamed. I started asking why not questions and completely trusted the answers I received.

Why Not?

As I began looking at what I believed to be true to maybe being untrue or at least a little warped I began experiencing something new. I started asking questions to a higher power. Some call this God, Source, The Universe, Jesus or guides. Who or what this entity is does not matter, I started seeking answers and actually got them. I began following guidance from this connection, even when I thought it was ridiculous, and there was always a great reason that I just didn't initially see. Because I actually had "results" I began looking even further and more deeply turning every rock I could upside down.

In my search for different perspectives, I started uncovering evidence that there is something more than what my logical mind believes is here. I am still logical, so my quest for answers had to hold up in this life I am in. I needed both belief and logic to hold hands.

I realized that mankind has believed in angels for eons. Many cultures around the world have art and history that references angelic beings even before these cultures connected with each other. Dragons are found in the mythologies of Europe, Asia, Africa, and the Americas long before commerce connected these cultures. If these exist around the world in various cultures as spirit protectors, then who has seen them and how? What if they do exist? Why not?

Some people believe in witches. In fact, these beings also are evident throughout history around the world. If these beings have been seen, then do they really exist as well?

And so on with elves, nymphs, fairies, and other creatures not evident in my physical experience.

And then I discovered the study of elementals. These are "creatures" that are made of the earth elements, Air, Water, Fire, and Water. Elements are the root of where "magic" comes from, and these elements appear in alchemical work, scientific studies, and folklore traditions.

Paracelsus, a German/Swiss physician, alchemist, and philosopher, wrote:

A Book on Nymphs, Sylphs, Pygmies, and Salamanders, and on the Other Spirits, in order to "describe the creatures that are outside the cognizance of the light of nature, how they are to be understood, what marvelous works God has created". He talks about elementals.

What you see and what you hear may not be what you get.

Because of this study I realized that my eyes did not see all that is there and sometimes I see what is there differently than others. For example, on a long drive I sometimes see the road moving under me rather than me driving over the road. It is how my brain interprets the data it receives from my eyes. Add to that, science has proven that we can only see 0.0035% of the visible light spectrum. And then, added to that, our ears pick up from 20 Hz up to 20,000 Hz frequency and our brain interprets what these frequencies mean. We do not pick up all vibrations, and we all interpret what we receive differently. Check out the Yanni vs Laurel audio test where, based on the frequency your eardrum picks up, you "hear" something different from the very same recording.

Here science has proven that there is so much more for us to understand if only we knew how to tap into it. What colors are there that we are not enjoying? What whispers are passing us by? What languages are being spoken that have died out or are not yet born? What music is being missed that could enrich our lives? How can we bring this richness and light into our experiences each day?

Why Dragons? Well, why not.

Dragons came into my life quite unexpectedly. In 2014, I was in the desert of Joshua Tree, CA on March 21 with some dear friends. That evening we rose, gave homage to the North, South, East, and West (elements of the earth) and held a small meditation. We were honoring the spring equinox and preparing for a 5-day spiritual retreat.

- East: New beginnings, birth, renewal, and the element of **Air**.
- South: Growth, warmth, summer, and the element of **Fire**.
- West: Introspection, the end of a cycle, maturity, and the element of **Water**.

- North: Wisdom, stability, winter, and the element of **Earth**.

I went back to bed to meditate, not realizing we had invoked the “elementals.”

Sometimes when meditating I have a visual place where I imagine myself on a beach relaxing and enjoying nature. I love the heat from the sun, the smell of the ocean, the sound of the waves, and the feeling of the sand. I went there in my mind that early morning in order to simply relax before we got up to head to the retreat we were there for.

In my “imagination” as I lay on the sand a dragon rose up from beneath me and took me on an amazing ride around the world. He was friendly, loving even, and his scales were soft and comfortable. His colors were deep and shimmering. I felt such love and affection from this creature I knew it had to be real. It felt like we knew each other from beyond time.

This got me thinking and, as I sometimes do, investigating. I now realize that dragons are also creatures that have been seen in cultures all around the world. So, I wonder, if they are evident in historic tales maybe there is more in this life than what I see or hear with my physical eyes and ears? Maybe there is so much more I can “see” and “hear” if I just allowed myself to believe these experiences to be true.

I began leaning into different approaches. I embraced meditation, speaking with angels, asking God for guidance, inviting God into my life and asking the question, "what can I do today to be even more aware of all that is not seen or heard with this physical body and understand the vastness of this universe?"

I got curious about energy, about quantum physics, and about following my "intuition." I took action on what I "heard" as guidance and what felt in alignment with my highest intention. I joined a group of intuitive women and began holding weekly dragon card readings and creating meditations supporting these creatures. The more I allowed my imagination to take over the more my experience became delicious. I heard dragon songs, felt the comfort of being held protectively by my dragon, and sunk deeply into loving profoundly and listening to direction from "the Gods" that made no sense.

I met with an energy healer who also channels information. He told me that I was in for a huge upgrade (stronger connection to that which we do not see) and another book was coming. Gawd, NOT ANOTHER BOOK!

And then I went on a road trip.

I literally felt my mind expanding as I drove along and had experiences that were not of this world. And yes, the plan for this book dropped like a ton of bricks into my mind. So, here I am, writing a book that is asking you, the reader, to embrace your imagination. Join me and live in a fantasy world for a bit and enjoy this collection of stories from a variety of dragons chosen from a deck of dragon oracle cards created by Diana Cooper. Each story stands on its own and talks about the dimensions of the dragon, who they are (thank you Diana) and the main character's experience with embracing them. They will fly, they will swim, they will travel the universe, and you will fall in love with these amazing elementals who have always been here, just like me, waiting for the chance to be seen, be loved, and be of service.

As a special bonus with these stories, I created meditations for each dragon allowing you to join interactively with each one. There are recordings, and the script outline for each mediation is in the Meditation section of this book.

Thank you for taking a chance and getting ready for magic, expansion, and love.

01 – Elementals and Dimensions

"There is no logical way to the discovery of these elemental laws. There is only the way of intuition, which is helped by a feeling for the order lying behind the appearance." - Albert Einstein

Embodying their elements, Earth is a towering figure made of stone and vines, Wind is an ethereal being with flowing robes and swirling air currents, Fire is a fierce figure wreathed in flames, and Water is a graceful, fluid form with waves and droplets. The background is a mystical landscape where all four elements converge in harmony.

Finding logic within the intuitive feeling of something existing beyond our known senses will take an act of trust and belief. Throughout the stories in Dragon Tails, you will hear me speak about the elementals and the dimensions related to these magical beasties.

Before I take you through this experience into your imagination I'd like to share a little bit about these very important reference points.

The Elementals

Why have you not seen these creatures? It is because these beasties are not evident to the naked eye and they are primarily made from the four basic elements of the world: earth, water, air, and fire. I have seen them as the force behind the patterns in my life. Something like guardian angels or spirit guides. They are there for me, always. I've learned to rely on them.

I invite you to lean into your imagination and allow yourself to get to know them a bit as we move on through these stories as each dragon we encounter is a combination of these elements.

Water

West: Introspection, the end of a cycle, and maturity.

Water is a conductor of energy, allowing the emotions I feel to move freely through me. With Water I can feel myself swimming in its flow as it holds the movement of my emotions, and I get to experience emotive healing, balance, intuition, creativity, and inner peace. When I am feeling hurt, confused, or out of sorts the water dragons come to my rescue.

Fire

South: Growth, warmth, and summer.

The burning flame of Fire is something I feel during change, transformation, and passion.

Comfort from fire shows up when I think of sitting around the campfire and sharing stories, roasting marshmallows, and poking the embers to keep warmth going.

I like to remind myself that I must learn to use my dragon's fire, so s/he warms me up at night while not burning down the village.

Everything fire has touched in my life has changed, sometimes beyond recognition, and ultimately for my benefit. Fire helps me alchemize and connect with my inner self.

Earth

North: Wisdom, stability, and winter.

The Earth elemental is ancient, deep, and unshakable. I believe that the times when I feel really anchored to the earth, smelling the dirt, and the aroma of fresh leaves are the moments I am with the earth elementals. Gaia consciousness holds ancient wisdom and brings me rationality and stability.

Invoking this elemental in my life can bring diligence and persistence but can also bring me stubbornly sticking to it. So, I look for the lesson, the security, and the wisdom being presented and then I know I must move on.

Air

East: New beginnings, birth, and renewal.

Air elementals remind me of fairies, the feeling of being free-spirited, and the moments of elusiveness. This element symbolizes communication, intelligence, and inspiration. Just like a breath of fresh air, this elemental clears the space for me with lightness and movement, it is a gateway to the Universe, and my life force energy.

The Dimensions

In science I learned about one, two, and three dimensions and in geometry or building something I can clearly rely on this knowledge. I've since learned that beyond these tangible realms that I experience in this world there are other densities, different frequencies. We are now going on an exploration together and are about to uncover some of the uniqueness of other dimensions. In these tales we touch on the 4th through the 9th dimensional dragons. There are many more dimensions, but the dragons that will be visiting us here are connected to the 4th, 5th, 7th, and 9th dimensions.

Personally, I experience these other dimensions as a "spiritual" state, an altered consciousness. This is a feeling, a knowing, and sometimes a vision or a voice that is not of this life. It is a combination of experiential occurrences, unexplained happenings, and profound belief that what I am touched by is real. When I am quiet, I can experience existing in many dimensions at the same time.

Fourth Dimension

An instant suspended in a quantum experience happens when I think of someone and the phone rings and it is them. I mention something at the same time someone else mentions it. I think of something or say something and then someone unrelated to that event repeats the very thought.

"Spooky happenings at a distance" occurs where anyone around the world can pick up my thoughts the moment I think them. These experiences are real and true and are not happening in this third-dimensional physical experience. But they are happening simultaneously.

I interact with the fourth dimension when my emotional awareness expands, maybe after meditation or simply after serious quiet times. A Sixth sense kicks in. It is here where synchronicities become normal. I lose all sense of time, not knowing what day it is or what time it is. I now also know that the fourth dimension is a bridge to other dimensions, a portal to the fifth.

Fifth Dimension

This is where I go to access Akashic records, my past, present, and future historical archives. This is the first level for me where the library of information for all time lies, and the front door opens to infinite possibilities. What is most relevant is when I am here, love is my state of being and I experience the underlying harmony in all existence. I see the essence of who you really are and in doing so, know the essence of me.

Sixth Dimension

The sixth dimension is the state where highly enlightened beings, or angels, exist. People who work with angels can access and interact in this dimension easily. Here is where I can perceive reality as multi-dimensional and my perspective expands to "knowing" profound truths, and I recognize a fundamental structure of existence, the game I call life.

Seventh Dimension

This is the realm of pure consciousness, transcending the limitations of form and time. This higher state of awareness acts as a portal where I have access to even higher realms of existence.

It is here where I find the "blueprint" that is me, my soul, my star-seed, my characteristics, and my belief patterns. This is also where I find that the framework of the stories of my incarnations had been defined. I am able to understand the purpose behind my earthly existence from this vantage point. This is a realm of spiritual planning and deep wisdom.

Eighth Dimension

From this vantage point I am able to perceive the fabric threads of the multiverse, multiple realities, and various timelines simultaneously. Here I am able to understand how each choice I make has a ripple effect and branches into different realities, creating a network of potentiality. I can perceive the intricate web of relationships that bind all living beings and the Universe itself together.

Ninth Dimension

This is a fun experience. It is here that I've met the intergalactic council. When I return from this experience, I can only remember a sense of what I "heard" but I still have a huge feeling that all that happened is understood. I have a knowing of the divine order underlying creation, and I find comfort in this knowledge. The pulse of all life resonates through me as a unified force, a oneness without separation, and shared moments with the Masters. I can glimpse the portal to even more from here and the wonders beckon me.

Our dragons have been created using one, two, or three elements. The beasties we will meet have originated from different dimensions and have been created to serve us, guide us, and support our evolution. When you want their assistance, you do not need to know which dragon to call on, but you do have to invite them in.

Join me as I invite some of them onto these pages. Meeting them just might change your life.

02 - Fourth Dimensional Dragons

"Through dominion in the fourth dimension - the realm of faith - you can give order to your circumstances and situations, give beauty to the ugly and chaotic, and healing to the hurt and suffering." — David Yonggi Cho

Imagine going beyond the three spatial references. Here I use vibrant gradients of blues, purples, oranges, and greens to symbolize the passage of time, with flowing ribbons or spirals that twist and fold into themselves. Include glowing nodes or orbs to represent moments in time, connected by luminous threads that weave through the structure.

"I feel," he said, "as if I had been wandering with Alice in Wonderland and had tea with the Mad Hatter." — Charles Lane Poor

The fourth dimension was my first step into the curious and wonderous world of imagination. This is a place I frequent as I imagine what tomorrow will bring or I remember what happened yesterday.

I invite you to come with me now to a land where mirrors live, facing each other, reflecting forward and backward all that ever was and all that ever will be, all at the same time.

In fact, there is no time constraint in this land. How normal is this thing we call time anyway?

I am here and I am everywhere, and all the answers can be found. In my mind I can think of many things simultaneously and these thoughts can be of any time or of no particular time indeed. When I go beyond the constraint of words and allow the feelings, colors, and music to take over, there are moments of magic and brilliance that move my soul. It's living without time constraints while feeling infinite possibilities leaking through. I can feel the experience, I know this intimately, and yet this is an encounter that is sometimes difficult to grasp.

Here there is no anger, no fear, no shame, and this is a place where I can learn to love myself, even while I observe all of my history and all of my potential futures. My heart feels free with the joy of non-judgment as I see life for what it is.

As I wander in this cloud of timelessness, the dragons from this fourth dimension take shape. These creatures in this dimension are simple in their beauty and their service for me and for you. Although they originate in the dimensional planes we cannot see, they come to us to support our experience in this life.

Let's touch on the past, present, and future of these beasties. They are here for us, and I have learned that they can only come when I welcome them in. Let me introduce you to a few I have met and feel free to invite one into your life.

03 - Earth Dragon

"But it is one thing to read about dragons and another to meet them." - Ursula K. Le Guin, A Wizard of Earthsea

The Earth Dragon is gracefully interacting with glowing Ley Lines that weave through the landscape, channeling magical energy. Around her is a lush, vibrant garden filled with blooming flowers, ancient stones, and mystical plants. The scene is bathed in warm, natural light, with a serene and magical atmosphere. The dragon appears wise and nurturing, harmonizing with nature and the energy of the Earth.

It was a perfect summer day, and I had some time to head off to the beach. I decided to rent a bicycle and ride around for a bit. I stopped by a sea wall, locked the bike, and went to a nearby stand for a bite to eat.

I sat on an open deck, facing the ocean while I ate. The breeze smelled of the sea, and the sun kissed my skin softly. After my meal I took some time to lay in the sand and watch the sun play across the sky, the birds swooped though the air, and the airplanes high above me glided by.

After a while I got on the bike to return it to the rental shop and decided to stop for a moment by a magnificent tree. I could smell its bark and feel its warmth as I leaned against it.

I sank down next to the trunk and for some reason I felt compelled to dig my fingers into the earth around me. When I looked down at my hands, I noticed the clawed feet of a dragon that was quietly standing next to me, watching over me like an angel.

When I first met this dragon her brown earth coloring was lined with a liquid-like blue energy that brought the smell of wet earth and the taste of nature to my mind. I could see her blue lines were feeding into the earth. Although this was a strange experience for me, I mean seriously, who sees dragons anyway, I found myself calmly asking her why she was here.

She told me she was here to speak with me about healing the earth by clearing the Ley Lines that hold Gaia together.

Being new to this interaction with dragons I was honest with my ignorance. I asked, “Pray tell, what are the Ley Lines?”

This Earth Dragon explained that there are key important monuments and landsites around the world that are interconnected with a sort of energetic highway that are called Ley Lines. When the world was constructed, Earth Dragons helped create the Ley Lines and this is why they are sometimes called Dragon Lines. These energy lines carry a powerful magnetic field that holds the earth together while simultaneously creating vortexes of energy centers around the world.

I mentioned that I had been to many sites where there were vortexes and I experienced psychic growth and met my first dragon in a meditation at one. This is the first time I have understood where these vortex energy centers came from. Many cultures around the world honor these as sacred sites.

The Earth Dragon shared the sadness she felt about the world and her concern about Gaia. These lines have not been honored or maintained. They have been injured due to war, neglect, mining, fracking, and misuse of the earth's resources. Earth Dragons, in fact all dragons, do not have free will. They must be invited in to do the work they have been created for. Therefore, the earth dragons have not been here often to tend to the lines.

I asked if I could see these lines and help heal them as I believed this is an important task indeed. The Earth Dragon got on her knees to allow me up on her back. She had a natural seat shape made of the blue energy that feeds the Ley Lines, and it fit me perfectly. We set off to inspect the lines.

As we flew along every once in a while, we would dip down, and the dragon would burn away some residue or calcification that was built up on a line or pour some healing blue essence into an injured line. I got off and helped clear away the residue left from our task.

At one point we were flying a bit low, and I felt a cold shiver go up my back. Have you ever walked into a place where it felt spooky and you just wanted to leave? There is a feeling of bad mojo someplace and you just need to get away.

Well, here we were at a place just like that. The Earth Dragon explained that sometimes negative energy or negative karma would get stuck in the earth and can be there for centuries. This could be a graveyard, a battlefield, or a place where horrible things happened, and the earth absorbed that essence and is unable to transmute it. I watched as the Earth Dragon carefully burned that energy away. She dug at the ground to get the energy to move and threw her flames so precisely, it was like a surgeon's scalpel removing the damage while saving the healthy body.

I could hear mother earth sigh with relief as we completed this task. We called down angels to help heal the wound left behind and invited other elementals to sing healing songs, shed healing light, and bestow healing balm restoring earth to a healthy state. I wondered, what can I do in my life now to help heal the damage mother earth must bear?

It was time to return, and the Earth Dragon flew me back to where we started. As I dismounted, I asked the dragon if I could call on her again. She told me she is the Earth Dragon and loves anything to do with this planet. I can call on her when I am ready to create a garden, be it fruit, vegetables, or flowering plants. She is here to create as well as heal. I can call on her any time, and she will help me plant and feed my garden whatever it needs.

I asked her to please keep working the Ley Lines. The fabric of this earth being maintained is important to me.

I kissed her forehead and thanked her for such a beautiful experience. I know I will ride with her again sometime and maybe we will dig in the dirt planting seeds in the warm sun someday soon.

04 - Fire and Water Dragon

"Personal growth is not a matter of learning new information but of unlearning old limits." - Alan Cohen

Watch as the colors transition from fiery reds, oranges, and golds on one side to cool blues, aquas, and silvers on the other. Its wings are large and ethereal, with one wing appearing like flames and the other like flowing water. The background is a cosmic, starry sky with hints of elemental energy swirling around. The dragon exudes a sense of wisdom, balance, and elemental harmony, with glowing eyes and a mystical aura.

After spending time with the Earth Dragon, I began to feel uneasy. Something was off. Something was ready to change. Something was calling me. I had no idea what, but I deeply felt it was time to let go and move on.

On this particular morning, I went to a service and there was a corral set up on the altar/stage with a horse inside. A gentleman dressed as a cowboy came onto the platform and told the audience this animal was three years old and had never been ridden. He was going to attempt to connect with her and ride her while sharing what was in his heart.

He entered the rink and proceeded to give a sermon about trust and love as he communicated with this remarkable beast.

He held her face, looked into her eyes, he stroked her while talking about connection and about love. Throughout, I felt pulled into the experience watching as one man changed everything from his heart. The horse slowly relaxed and began to allow this man to mount, get off, stroke her some more, then mount and get off again. All the while speaking about surrender, trust, love and leading from his heart.

The choir began to sing, and this man knelt before the horse and looked into her eyes with love. She looked back. They were quiet and still. Together they exchanged their hearts through the entire song, he did not say a word, and the audience wept. The horse finally allowed this man to mount her and be gently led around the rink as the only thing she needed in order to build trust was love.

During this experience I heard "Let me in." I looked around and wondered, "let who in for what?" When this sermon was over, I strolled out to the parking lot. I was deep in thought and very much moved from this experience of love. When I got outside, I heard the swoosh of powerful wings and there she was before me. A powerful orange and green dragon. I looked around to see if anyone else noticed this event. Apparently, it was just me.

There was an overpowering sense of love coming from this creature. Like the cowboy I just observed. I then knelt down before her, looked into her eyes, and asked who she was.

"I am a Fire-and-Water dragon, and I am here because you are ready to make changes in your life. I heard your call today, coming from your heart. I asked you to let me in. I am here to help you clear the way."

She was right. So much was shifting in my life, and I felt fear about the unknown, I felt stuck about my current life, I felt blinded by the unforeseen. I believed that I did need help in moving forward and I wanted to let the heart of this magnificent creature in.

The Fire and Water dragon was here to help me feel calm, believe in love, and trust that my path would be clear. She reminded me that I am never alone and all I need in my life is available to me simply by asking.

I took a deep breath, shook out my nerves and intentionally relaxed each muscle from the top of my head out through my toes. I took deep and slow breaths and slowed down the noise in my head. In this moment I knew I was like the horse I just witnessed, and the Fire and Water dragon was the cowboy ready to lead me where I needed to go.

I mounted the dragon, and we flew above the world, moving from continent to continent, from hemisphere to hemisphere, and from this vantage point the world seemed beautiful and safe. We witnessed storms and quiet. We saw oceans, lakes, rivers, streams. We flew over mountains and deserts, cities, and farmland. And we finally landed on a mountain top that arose out of the ocean just for us.

As I dismounted, the dragon shared some thoughts with me.

"As you observed the world you noticed extremes. There were areas of chaos and areas of peace and everything in between. Balance is like standing in the middle of a seesaw. There is a sway that happens, and you must look at both sides of a sway and acknowledge them both. No judgment and no conclusions.

I am both fire AND water. Why does the fire not evaporate the water or the water quench the fire? I am in balance. I have a balanced mind, body, and spirit and look at both sides of a situation. The Universal Law of Polarity shows me how to be flexible with my thoughts and beliefs. This is a life of contrast and polarity tells me that with contrast I gain clarity. Tuning into what the opposite looks like can reveal a new perspective or lesson.

You are about to experience the magic this creates."

I sat before this elemental and went into a trance. As she sang her ethereal song, I watched, in my mind's eye, as she began burning. I watched old stories that were holding me back go up in flames, creating a clear path for me to move forward. Old relationships melted away. Old wounds cauterized and closed up. Old thoughts of who I thought I was turned to ash and blew away. A whole new world began to open up before me, and it was magnificent.

I felt the ebb and flow of water wash over me, allowing my senses, long in a dormant state, to come alive again as I let go, and released resistance and began to go with the flow of what was coming.

What happened next is that the Fire and Water dragon combined these two elements, creating steam all around me and through me. I felt the power push behind me giving me the energy, determination, and belief I needed to take action. I felt the steam cleaning what was left inside of me. I felt the lightness that came as I became one with the steam.

And then her song stopped. She began to gently hum, bringing my consciousness back.

As I opened my eyes I looked back into the eyes of this dragon, and I saw excitement, joy, and laughter. She was propelling me forward on my ascension path. The stories that were anchoring me down were in the past and it was time for me to play, to remember, and to awaken. It was delicious. We danced, we laughed, and we created circles of light as I embraced this day anew.

I mounted the Fire and Water dragon and as we arose, I watched as the mountain we were on return to the ocean floor and we headed home. When I got off, I knew I had changed, I had become something more.

I felt my body all tingly and there was a love-power in my heart. I looked at this life I had chosen from a space of joy, and I knew absolutely everything had changed in the most joyous way.

I thanked the Fire and Water dragon for hearing me and coming when I called and I look forward to now living from a different vibration and to living a life full of magic.

05 - Fire Dragon

“All the records of your past lives are contained within your own mind, just as the records of your ancestors are contained within your DNA. “- Frederick Lenz

A majestic red and orange fire dragon with a gentle and serene expression, gracefully flying through a mystical landscape. The dragon is surrounded by swirling flames that are not destructive but purifying, as it burns away dark, shadowy negative energy fields. The atmosphere is magical and peaceful, with glowing embers and soft light illuminating the scene. The dragon's scales shimmer with warmth and kindness, and its eyes reflect wisdom and compassion.

What a remarkable transformation after spending time with the Fire and Water dragon. I was taking a long drive and feeling my brain tingle as new ideas and inspiration came pouring in. I felt excited and looked forward to what might be coming next, and then something strange happened.

As I drove over the road the vision in front of me changed from the road to that of a city. I took my hand and pushed this scene aside while thinking, "I'm driving. You can't be in my way." The image appeared again, this time more clearly. Once more I pushed it aside. The third time this came up I moved it over saying, "I am in this reality right now. You need to stay out of my way."

That evening, as I settled down for the night, I thought about this recurring image and wondered what it might be. As I slipped into *hypnagogia*, the transitional state of consciousness between wakefulness and sleep, I began having visions of this city's scape. I was living there, and the experience was vivid and very real. When

I woke the next morning, the only thing I could remember was how deeply sad and afraid I felt.

After the clearing I had recently experienced, this felt heavy and was something I couldn't quite grasp. I asked, "How can I understand what is happening to me and how do I address it?"

As I walked toward my vehicle I looked up at the puffy clouds in the sky and noticed that one cloud was moving toward me and changing color as it got closer. This creature was turning shades of red and orange and was clearly becoming a dragon.

As he landed in front of me, we shared a moment of greeting. I was getting used to these creatures showing up but did look around to see who was in the parking lot with me witnessing this event. I was alone.

I thanked the dragon for coming to me and asked what we would be doing. He introduced himself as a Fire Dragon. His expertise is that of clearing. He explained that fire is a powerful element for purification and release. He rolled up in the grass beside me and invited me to lay down beside him. We were going on a quest to the past, beyond today and into a history I had forgotten.

I got comfortable snuggling up against his warm dragon body, I felt the ebb and flow of his breathing. I could hear the rhythm of his heart. I was lulled by the music of his voice as he began in a sing-song manner talking to me.

“You, my dear, are a product of your past lives. Some of these experiences empower you and others weigh you down. The light of the flames from my fire will shine a light on the darkness that you are feeling, the negative energetic charge you do not even realize is present. These are shadows of fear and pain from past incarnations that are showing up for you as throat problems, stomach issues, and focus disruption in this lifetime.

Walk down the path in front of you as I burn those stuck energies for you. Feel your body let go as you are now able to release these energetic statements and inspire new and healthier visions for your future to emerge.

Feel yourself experiencing even more confidence and courage as we release you from the energetic stories of past challenges, allowing you to move forward with faith.”

The dragon told me I was on a soul level adventure of continual enlightenment, and he offered to protect me with a wall of Etheric fire. I agreed that this would be very beneficial and very much appreciated. I asked. “Would you create this protection around me, my home, and my loved ones as well?”

He began to direct his fire at everything I asked him to clear, transmuting lower vibrations into higher frequencies and creating a wall of protection against energy no longer aligned to my highest good.

The Fire Dragon placed a wall of etheric fire around my aura, warding off any negative energy that may come my way while he cleared a path in front of me.

This Fire Dragon was clearing my soul pathway, burning up unnecessary challenges before I reached them.

When he was done, the Fire Dragon gently nudged me to open my eyes and take a deep breath. His voice was deep and soothing. His eyes were full of confidence and knowing. I stretched as I rose up and felt lighter. There was a feeling of knowing something I had not yet understood as well as an airiness within me that was never evident before. I had changed.

"You are now able to experience the moment you are in without the cloudiness from past experiences." He was softly whispering in my ear. "Be diligent and intentional about embracing the now and you will find answers in the space between your breaths."

I offered the dragon a white rose and thanked him for showing me something I didn't quite understand. As the dragon left, flying into the clouds, his color melted away until he was once more transformed into a cloud.

I got into my car and realized that barely a moment had passed in this interchange between the Fire Dragon and me. I was so grateful for this loving experience and for the clarity this cleansing brought to this moment in my life.

As I drove away, I could hear the dragon's voice in my head telling me. "You are not alone. Fire Dragons are always available, and we want you to feel happy and safe. Go ahead and ask us to protect and inspire you as well as your loved ones anytime you feel the need for clearing."

I could feel them with me, and it was good to know that this is so.

06 – Fifth Dimensional Dragons

"We have lived alongside higher frequencies for decades, the angelic realms, plus many other high frequency beings have communicated with us throughout history but the significance of their messages have frequently remained misunderstood."
- Jennifer Lynch (5th Dimensional Earth)

A surreal 5th-dimensional visualizing the quantum interpretation paradox. The image depicts multiple overlapping realities and timelines, represented as translucent, interwoven geometric planes and spheres. The overall tone is mysterious, thought-provoking, and abstract, with a color palette of deep blues, purples, and golds.

Quantum interpretations

Every quantum event branches into all possible outcomes, each realized in a separate, parallel universe.

We are now moving past the Fourth Dimension which serves as a portal to the next frequency, the Fifth Dimension. This is the realm of love and compassion. Many of the dragons from this frequency work with the Archangels and help in shifting human consciousness. This is where the Universal Law of Polarity no longer exists. It is where we experience the transcending of dualities. In this new perspective, love and God-centered choices take precedence over egoic desires. In fact, there is no egoic desire.

Fifth Dimensional Dragons play a key role in our planetary ascension and connecting with them help to unlock your spiritual eyesight.

I welcome you to join me as we get a chance to step into the knowing of ancient wisdom from these magnificent beings as well as experience healing your body and so much more. It's time to remember that humans once walked beside dragons and they are anxiously waiting for us to do so again.

07 - Black Dragon from Saturn

"Not all men were meant to dance with dragons." – George R.R. Martin, A Dance with Dragons

A majestic black dragon from Saturn, sitting gracefully on one of Saturn's icy rings. She is enormous, as tall as three men, with a muscular, sleek body covered in deep black scales that shimmer faintly with cosmic light. Her wings are vast, spanning the length of her body, folded elegantly around her. Her face is angelic, with delicate features and glowing eyes that radiate ancient wisdom. The backdrop features the gas giant Saturn with its swirling clouds and other rings in the distance, set against the starry void of space.

After going through the clearing experiences with dragons, I was feeling light, as though a cool breeze was now running through my body. I lived like this for several weeks and I observed changes in my life as a result of my perspective having shifted.

I was feeling a sense of love that filled my heart, filled my body, and overflowed to fill the room I was in. In my observations I asked questions rather than making assumptions. What else, what if, what more, and so on. I saw shades of colors never before evident. I smelled the essence of nature wherever I went. I tasted the sweetness of the air and of the earth and knew it had always been there. My senses were heightened, and I was listening even more intensely.

And I heard voices, guidance, in my mind. Sometimes a whisper and other times quite clear. We bantered. One day I asked, "Is this me, my ego, talking or is this you?" The response I got was, "Does it even matter?" From this interaction I learned to stop trying to understand and categorize and just trust from my heart.

And so, on this late spring morning while visiting the high desert, I took a morning walk. I found a trail that led away from the homes and followed it. As my mind wandered, I felt a deep longing for more. The changes I experienced and the magic I witnessed stirred a type of hunger within me. There was a knowing that this was just the beginning.

"What more can I do right now to allow the wisdom I know that is available to pour into me, allowing me to show up in this world as a beacon of truth, a lighthouse of guidance for seekers looking for The Way, their way, home?"

As I finished this question in my mind, I looked down the path I was walking on and saw boldly standing there a beautiful black dragon. She was waiting for me to approach. She was huge, she was majestic, and she was wonderous.

As I got closer, I could see the muscles in her legs pulse with strength. Her wings were long, spanning her entire body, and moved with the grace of a dance. Her color was so deep it shimmered, and I could get lost in its hue. When I reached her, I noticed that my head barely reached slightly passed what would be the knee of her front leg. I felt small but I also felt curious.

I greeted her, "Good morning beautiful beast. May I know who you are?"

She responded, "Good morning to you as well. I am one of the many Black Dragons of Saturn. I heard you calling me to guide you onto your next evolution of growth and expansion."

"How so?" I asked.

"You just asked a powerful question seeking guidance and knowledge. If you are looking for answers, I invite you to climb aboard, and we will begin your next lesson together."

I was even more curious now and ready for something new. I hiked myself up upon her back and sank into a feathery nest of comfort. Her powerful legs pushed off, and we took flight. Her wings shot us upward with a speed I could not describe. I was shocked to see we were leaving Earth and that I was not affected at all. We left the atmosphere and glided into space. Together, we flew past the Moon, swung by Mars, took a right at Jupiter, and then softly landed on a moon within one of the rings of Saturn.

I was surprised to realize that this was a rather loud place to be.

The data gleaned from [2]Cassini's instruments allowed researchers to listen to and analyze the patterns of

---

[2] Cassini is the Cassini-Huygens mission, a collaborative space mission between NASA and the European Space Agency (ESA). The mission

these emissions. One thing uncovered was revealing how Saturn's auroras are similar to Earth's northern and southern lights. The emissions are more than just a cosmic phenomenon; they are keys to unlocking the mysteries surrounding the interactions between the planet's atmosphere and its space environment. Investigating Saturn's radio emissions not only enriches our knowledge of the ringed planet but also contributes to the broader exploration of space. The study of the planet's subtle, complex emissions strengthens our grasp of planetary science within our solar system.

I could see the rings around Saturn, and they were ethereal, delicate, and light. They seemed almost perfect. There were many moons around this planet and Saturn itself was quite colorful.

Her shades were different than colors from Earth, I would say a mixture of yellow, gold, and brown, with hints of blue, white, and orange. Her atmosphere was quite stormy. I could feel the energy of this tumultuous activity even here on a moon-planet within her rings.

The Black Dragon of Saturn had me dismount and as I was climbing down she told me Saturn's moons hold secrets to the origins of life. "We will wait for the

---

included the Cassini orbiter, the first spacecraft to orbit Saturn, and the Huygens probe, which successfully landed on Titan, Saturn's largest moon

Masters to appear while you practice focus, concentration, determination, and heightened awareness."

Saturn was also one of the Gods in ancient Rome and played a role in Roman mythology. Saturn was described as a god of time, generation, dissolution, abundance, wealth, agriculture, periodic renewal, and liberation. Saturn's mythological reign was depicted as a Golden Age of abundance and peace. My imagination created scenarios as to what living under this protection might have been like.

I sat quietly while observing the beauty of this scenery and felt an abundance of love pouring from the heart of this dragon. Shortly, I heard a voice say, "Come on in. We are waiting for you."

I looked up and saw a crystal building with a gem lined walkway leading to its door. The Black Dragon of Saturn explained, "This is one of [3]Seraphina's Intergalactic training establishments in the inner planes." She was at the door greeting me to come in. Half dragon and half human-like, her words seemed to emanate a fiery glow.

As I entered, I noticed the council sitting in a circle. I was invited to enter the inner circle and sit on a soft cushion

---

[3] The name Seraphina in Hebrew means "fiery ones" or "burning ones." Derived from the Hebrew word for seraphim, celestial beings with six wings and symbolizing purity and divine love.

of dragon feathers. As I sat there, I could hear them all speak in a language I had never heard before, yet it was familiar, and I understood their meaning.

I realized I was being Attuned to Seraphina's frequency. A beam of light from her eyes entered my Third eye. It felt warm and inviting and the frequency I felt brought goosebumps to my body. It seemed only a moment passed and we were done. Seraphina placed a six-pointed star crystal into my open crown.

I was invited to stand and as I was leaving, I heard, "You are now ready for intergalactic service. Working with Seraphina and the Intergalactic Council you are invited to work with us and open a Stargate to assist with decisions being made for earth's future."

I wondered, "What does that even mean?"

The Black Dragon of Saturn greeted me at the door and told me we had one more stop to make. I mounted her again and she took me to her home planet, Saturn. There we entered a castle carved into a mountain of gold, green, and grey.

Waiting for us inside was Archangel St. Germain. This angelic being lived on earth many times. His reincarnation is over now as he had been freed from the rounds of rebirth in a ritual of the ascension. He had transcended.

He greeted me, explaining, "I won my freedom from mortal incarnations and justifications of an existence outside the One. I'd like you to understand that you are mortal and that I am immortal. The only difference between us is that I have chosen to be free, and you have yet to make that choice."

He continued, "Here you will learn the founding principles of magical intergalactic travel. You will learn that your quest is just as important as your destination. Maybe even more so. I am a master alchemist and bestow upon you the gift of the violet flame of freedom, thus awakening the alchemist within you."

As I sat bathed in this flame that felt warm and inviting, my attunement had me merge with St. Germain's energy, and this continued until our frequency vibrated together as one. In that moment I understood what true freedom feels like.

When we were done St, Germain told me that I am on my ascension path now and will build my life from a state of love, from the heart, and for the highest good of all.

I thanked St, Germain for this most generous gift. I was speechless and in awe.

I mounted the Black Dragon of Saturn, and we returned to Earth. She landed exactly where we began. As I dismounted, she congratulated me. I passed a tremendous test, and it was time to celebrate my success and step forward with joy and bliss.

I watched the Black Dragon of Saturn fly away. I turned on my path and headed home wondering how my life was going to unfold after all that had transpired. What more lies before that is full of wonder and of the highest good to all? In that moment I knew my adventures had just begun.

08 - Green Dragon

"I believe in everything until it's disproved. So, I believe in fairies, the myths, dragons. It all exists, even if it's in your mind. Who's to say that dreams and nightmares aren't as real as the here and now?" - John Lennon

A serene green dragon sitting gently on a rock that juts out from a lush forest landscape. The dragon's scales resemble intertwining vines, blending naturally with the woodland surroundings. She has a delicate wild-flower tattoo on her leg, and beside her lies a gold and green key, glinting softly in the dappled sunlight filtering through the trees. The atmosphere is peaceful and magical, with soft moss, ferns, and wildflowers dotting the forest floor.

I woke up one morning feeling like something had deeply changed. I can only explain what I felt. There was an expansion in my brain, like something was happening all around and deeply within. There was a love in my heart that took my breath away and it was palatable. There were tears in my eyes as I thought of all that was changing and how I am so fortunate that I have been selected to interact with the dragons.

Who knew?

I got up, made a cup of coffee, and sat down to gaze out the window. The tree limbs were gently moving in the breeze. The leaves were dozens of shades of green. The sun shone through softly brushing each tree and the landscape took my breath away. In that moment, I felt the presence of something greater than myself.

I decided that today would be a very good day to take a walk in nature; someplace with trees and birds and such. So, I proceeded to get changed, grabbed some water, and headed to a local wooded trail.

The path I selected was about two miles long and went down to a lake then back up to where I parked. It was short enough to enjoy and deep enough into the woods to forget about civilization.

I love the smell of pine needles in nature; it touches my soul. As I strolled along breathing in this essence, I saw fern, moss, holly-leaf and so much more. I heard birds chirping, watched a fox stop, look at me, then continue on, and then I noticed a deer munching quietly, look up at me, then scamper away. Each detail of the scene shimmered with a quiet, breathtaking grace. As I turned around a bend I noticed an owl in a tree.

I stopped and watched as he watched me. We seemed to commune together. I wondered why he was awake midday, and he wondered why I cared. It was hilarious. As I chuckled at this mental interaction I heard a rustle behind me.

I turned, and there gently sitting on a rock jutting out of the landscape sat a beautiful green dragon. She had scales that looked like vines, a wild-flower tattoo on her leg, and a gold and green key by her side. Her very breath sounded like the wind rustling the brush around us.

I was no longer surprised at these random encounters. Dragons were becoming quite normal to me now. The unusual becoming usual.

We greeted each other.

I bowed my head and said, “Hello there. You are gorgeous. It is so very nice to meet you.”

The Green Dragon regally looked at me and replied, “Good day and thank you for calling me in. I am thrilled to share the wonders of this forest with you and help you unlock sacred secrets and connect with nature. You see, you are one with all that is around you. It feeds you and you feed it. I invite you now to come walk with me and observe.”

My curiosity was piqued, I felt myself being pulled, wanting to know more. And so, I stepped off the path and into the woods with the Green Dragon.

She was here to invite me to understand who she was, what nature really is, and to open up my mind to what has always been right in front of me, in fact, right inside of me all along. The question of “who am I” was about to be unfolded.

She explained that as the Green Dragon, she represents nature’s protector and the is integral to the interconnectedness of life. She works with the planet. She spoke to me about Gaia’s consciousness and how she is alive, breathing, and a *sentient being*. The Earth is focused on creating an environment that is optimal for life. She has a purpose and is connected to the plants, the animals, the earth, and to me. We are all unique and serve the purpose of supporting this planet. This remarkable creature reminded me of the importance of preserving Gaia and learning to listen to her ancient wisdom.

The Green Dragon continued her story in order for me to better understand her.

She can only be found in the deepest, darkest parts of the forest and, like me, loves the peace of solitude. She is pure power and strength and embodies the essence of nature and its cycles. The rhythm of nature, the rhythm of the earth's cycles, and the rhythm of our bodies are all connected. She emphasized that she does not appear to just anyone, she selects with extreme discernment, appearing only to those who are authentic and on the quest of connection and oneness and only when their desire for more calls to her.

I felt so honored to be walking with her through her domain. I listened to her guidance very closely as her voice was like a whisper and had music to it that soothed my heart.

She explained we are all made up of sacred geometry and wanted me to connect with that within mother nature.

"Notice the plants around you. When you look closely you can see repeating patterns that form geometric shapes. These patterns hold symbolic and spiritual significance as this is sacred geometry. These create the blueprint of life on this earth. You too are made up of sacred geometry, and these are the keys to unlocking within you the answers you seek.

These shapes create a frequency and emit energy. They draw what each being needs and emit that which supports other life forms. For example, let us look at the Fibonacci sequence here in nature that creates an ever-expanding spiral. It is a series of numbers where each subsequent number is the sum of the two preceding ones: 0, 1, 1, 2, 3, 5, 8, 13 and so on. Plants exhibit the Fibonacci sequence in leaves, petals, and seeds.

Take a look at this sunflower, the number of spirals formed by the seeds on a sunflower head align with the Fibonacci sequence. This geometry has a sequence that allows each seed to receive an equal amount of sunlight and water. Nature living by a divine geometric blueprint.

And so do you.

The sacred geometry in nature is made up of fractals; therefore, they are infinite. These self-repeating patterns mirror the world of nature, which you are a part of. I am here to help you understand beauty and your connection to nature and how sacred geometry governs you and the universe."

I was speechless after this. I thought, “Sacred geometry is within me? I am part of nature?” I always understood this on an intellectual basis but now I could feel it. I was overcome with how I was connecting to everything around me. It may not make sense to you, but I felt as if my body and spirit, in that moment, were melting into the scenery around me.

The Green Dragon now had a huge grin on her face as she watched me become what she was talking about. “I want you to enjoy this experience right now as you understand how you are one with this beauty and balance. Feel this emanate throughout your body as you tune in to the sacred geometry within you and everywhere in nature.”

When she finished, I felt aligned, whole, and healed. I had not even realized how unbalanced and mis-aligned I had been. I now felt vibrant and vibrating. I felt alive and exalted. I saw this life like I had never seen it before. I could feel the consciousness of Gaia reaching up to touch my toes. It was magic.

As I looked at the Green Dragon with her vines, tattoo, and key, I noticed her fading away, melting back into the surrounding scenery. She was returning to her solitude as her role was done. I thanked her, I thanked the trees, I thanked the plants, I thanked the earth and everything she stands for as I realized I am a part of all of this. I am deeply rooted in the ebb and flow of this planet while simply a temporary vessel created from love to experience what I observe each and every moment.

As I walked back to the parking lot, I could barely touch the ground. The sun was dancing for me, the animals sang for me, the air embraced me, and everything began to make a different kind of sense. Once again, I had been changed. I was connected to an ancient consciousness that guided each step I took.

Gaia and I are one.

09 - Golden Christed Dragon

"Above us, outlined against the brilliant sky, dragons crowded every available perching space on the Rim. And the sun made a gold of every one of them." —Anne McCaffrey, Nerilka's Story

A majestic Christ dragon perched gracefully on a high mountain ledge. The dragon is entirely golden, with shimmering scales. She has expansive, majestic golden wings folded elegantly at her sides. Her long, golden tail curls around the ledge, glinting in the sunlight.

It had been a month since I last saw and interacted with a dragon. I could feel their presence around me all day long and I heard their wings in the breeze when I went for a walk. But to see them again, to talk with one, to share the energy transmitted, ah, this was something I was deeply missing. How odd to think that these "mystical" creatures have become an important part of my life.

I loved exploring my connection to nature now and the dragons have become an important part of that experience. As I was contemplating how I was feeling I asked myself, "what more mysteries can I be shown?" I realized that missing these conversations was something new to me. I have always been comfortable being in my own company and also loved sharing space with others.

When spending time alone, I go on thought journeys exploring the galaxy both beyond this planet, within this earth, and in my body. These experiences that I can create filled me with joy. So, this gap I was feeling with missing dragon encounters was something to be curious about.

I began asking myself what was I feeling? Where was I feeling it? How can I release any pressure holding my emotion back, allowing it to rise and present itself to me? As I asked these questions, I realized that my birthday was in two days. I was so involved in all that had been happening I had lost all sense of time.

So, what do I want for my birthday? I didn't want a thing. I wanted a feeling. I wanted to experience expansive love and share this with the world. I know this might sound a bit unusual, but I needed nothing and wanted to share deeply. Is it possible to love so profoundly that my heart's overflow can change the world?

As I asked myself more and more questions, I sat on the deck in the back of my house on an Adirondack chair built specifically for me. It fit me perfectly and was a place I'd go to when I wanted quiet and nature time and to breathe in the fresh air.

I believe I dozed off thinking about a conversation I had once with my dear spiritualist friend. In this discussion he told me that I would receive the Christ Energy after going through a particular process in my life. This experience he foretold had happened, and it had changed my perspective on reality completely. Now, especially because of the impact of the Dragon visits, I feel a profound sense of love, soul-connection, and surrender, knowing that I am now able to make my choices from Joy and Love.

This feeling, this Christ Energy, is something we all have access to. We simply have to release enough of our past baggage, leaving the stories behind, to be able to allow this deep energy in. I have certainly left much of my history back where it belongs. Now, while in my dream state I heard a whisper, "The Truth." As I began to wake up, I remembered hearing this and it reminded me that I had studied the Kabbalah, The Tree of Life, and Patterns on The Trestleboard, where I explored the statement, "This is the Truth about life." I wondered, is that The Truth from my dream?

And then I saw her.

Actually, I felt her presence long before seeing her. This dragon had an aura of love and light so expansive that I could feel it at least 500 meters away. When I saw her perched on my balcony, she was totally gold, she sported golden-shield-like scales on her chest that were anchored near her heart space with a golden stone that emanated rays of golden light and created a feeling of love. She was proud and she was bold.

She took my breath away.

My heart raced with excitement, and I smiled at her. She nodded at me and began to speak. "I am called the

Golden Christed Dragon. I have arrived to gift you access to a higher love so that you not only have access to the Christ Energy but actually embody the Christ Light.

I came to you from the heart of the Celestine Expanse, the realm where the veil between the divine and the earthly realm is quite thin. I was born from the breath of the Creator and the first golden dawn. There I walked the Golden Dawn path and underwent an initiation of a ritual death and rebirth, until my masks were stripped away, and only the eternal spark of the Christ Light remained. I am the embodiment of divine love, radiant truth, and eternal light."

She continued with a voice dreams are made of, "My Heart-stone embedded in my chest, anchored near my heart space, is a luminous gem that pulses with golden rays that stretch across valleys, mountaintops, rivers, oceans, in all that I can see, casting compassion, warmth, and serenity over all who come near."

"I am unwavering truth, and my voice resonates like a celestial bell, clear, and commanding. My love is so pure it dissolves hatred and is a light so strong it reveals truth."

I was curious now. Me? I am being gifted with this amazing love. I felt humbled, awed, and tearful. I asked, "How will this be accomplished."

Her response was surprising, “It has already begun. The light rays I have bestowed upon you contain Quantum Dragon Energy. This energy is reaching into the very cells of your body and re-programming each one with Golden DNA Light Codes. Each code will open up in its own time presenting you with the wisdom of creation and the coded frequency of Christ Love.”

I could feel myself absorbing the Christ Light she was sharing with me. I felt warmth, I felt loved, I felt protected. I also knew at a deep level that I could easily share this with the world. In fact, I felt compelled to bring this experience forward for others to understand who they truly are. I was being pulled toward a destiny unknown.

I felt the pull of a divine mission. I heard a soft voice in my head telling me, “You are loved, you are protected with the True light, and you will never walk in spiritual darkness again.”

I fell to my knees and looked into the Golden Christed Dragon’s eyes. “I have no words that could ever express how much gratitude and love I have for this moment today.” She responded, “I came when you were ready. Now you can pass love, healing, and wisdom on to others as you now radiate the golden energy of the Christ. You also have the wisdom and discernment to know when someone is ready for this gift.”

With that, she softly turned around and flew away leaving streams of golden light in her path.

I now knew how profoundly my destiny was changing. There was something more yet to come and I looked forward to embracing it all. This experience that I call life is unfolding in a very different way. It seems that the more "knowing" I encounter the more "unknowing" I become.

10 - Orange Dragon

"If the sky could dream, it would dream of dragons."
— Ilona Andrews

The Orange Dragon has a long, winding tail, holding a soft glowing orange sun. The sun emits radiant orange rays, casting a warm glow on the dragon's shimmering scales. The dragon has a majestic and slightly whimsical appearance.

After my encounter with the Golden Christed Dragon, I felt very centered, grounded, and connected to our source all at the same time. I became more contemplative than usual and was holding full conversations with myself in my mind. I believe I was speaking with the Angels, the Councils, and the Universe all concurrently and yet not confusingly. I was getting direction, information, insight, and feeling trancelike at times. My brain tingled, my heart palpitated, my ability to express what I was becoming physically, mentally, and emotionally fell short. I could find no words to describe what was happening and how I had changed.

The days slipped by and then here I was again at service listening to a sermon that was all about wisdom vs knowledge. On this day I was listening to a Lay Minister speak about King Solomon. He reminded us that when asked what he wanted Solomon chose discernment. The response he received from God was, “I will give you a wise and discerning heart, so that there will never have been anyone like you, nor will there ever be.”

I listened to this discussion on surrendering control, embracing trust, distinguishing wisdom vs knowledge, spending time on reflection, listening to each other, and most importantly, listening to the Universe and feeling in alignment with the choices we make. I looked around at the people in the pews, and it seemed that these words drew some people together. I also noticed as I looked around that some people were missing this deep and moving lesson as they appeared distracted or unmoved. I looked within myself and found that I felt alone in this sea of people. Isolated within my own experience. Who here would comprehend the connection I now felt with dragons and the trust I have in the messages I have been receiving?

I headed home and took the dog outside to play, and then we hung around in the yard for a bit. I was contemplating the lessons I heard and sincerely felt that there is no one quite like me. Just as there is no one like anyone else on this planet. It felt both magical and isolating. I had no one I could talk to about what I was experiencing, and I felt alone.

And then, I noticed a hummingbird fly by and land on a bush near me, turn around, and very intentionally she hovered there as she was watching me. She stayed there the whole time I was out and watched what I was doing, intensely curious. This is unusual for me to see a hummingbird stay and watch me for any length of time.

I felt honored for this moment. There seemed to be a connection I was hungry for that was now being met and I was grateful.

Later, at sunset, I looked over at the mountains and saw soft puffy clouds lingering gently over the hills. The sun shone through them and in between them I could see the light rays passing through, making strips of silver against the sky. The reflection seemed to be shimmering and moving toward me. As it got closer its colors changed and became distinct and there was no mistake, this was an orange dragon coming my way.

He gently landed next to me on my front lawn. I briefly wondered if the neighbors were watching and if they were, what must they be thinking. He spoke to me in a deep rhythmic language that was not of this earth. Strangely, I not only felt what he was saying, I completely understood it. This language sounded familiar, and it felt comfortable.

“You have awoken spiritually to a level where you can no longer forget who you are. Right now, many people are confused by your changes, and you are feeling alone. You have summoned me as you desire connection with community, and I am here to bring you this and more.”

I invited the Orange Dragon in, but he chose to lead me to the back where I had seen the hummingbird. We sat together on the deck, and it felt so right.

"My mission is to help soul-communities find each other. There is a certain frequency you are vibrating at now and you seem out of phase with those not yet awake. I am connected with the Archangel Metatron, and his energy and guidance is supporting us. Feel the change within you as I pour high frequency light into your aura to attract the attention of the masters, and elementals who are guiding you."

I then felt a warm glow around my navel, and it created a ripple throughout my body that lit up all my senses. It was a joy and pleasure I have never felt before.

"If you choose you can call on me, the Orange Dragon, to help you connect and build community. With the warmth of the sun now emanating from within you we can move forward to creating a unified world guided by the Masters. You can be part of creating a new world."

I sat there stunned. I understood that I was changing with each dragon encounter. I realized that I saw life differently as I alchemized into something, someone, I was not before. I had acquired a perspective and a knowing that was unlike my previous life beliefs. But to be an agent of change? To be part of unifying the world? To be someone who builds communities.

I was amazed.

I assured the Orange Dragon that I would be calling on him for guidance, and I was ready and willing to work with him to create an impact in this world that brings people together in love and harmony. I simply needed some time to absorb what this all means and allow my head to stop spinning.

I had no idea how this would be achieved but the feeling I had was electrifying and I knew there was a vision now planted in my mind, a program to become engaged, that had to happen. It was growing and it was crystal clear.

"I will see you soon," sang the Orange Dragon as he softly pushed off and flew back into the sun rays dancing between the clouds.

I remained on my deck for several hours, though it felt like just a moment. I was ecstatic and I was lit up. This life of mine was changing quickly and the anticipation of what would come next was palpable.

I don't believe I slept that night as this encounter replayed in my mind, my body, and my very soul over and over again. I wondered what would happen next.

11 - Magenta Dragon

"We often look for truth behind the veil of illusion, where reality collides with dreams." - A. M. Homes

A beautiful, elegant magenta dragon with a long, curling tail that forms the shape of an infinity symbol. The dragon has slender, curled-back horns like those of a ram, extending gracefully along her long neck. Her eyes radiate wisdom, and she wears a knowing grin. The overall aesthetic is majestic and graceful, with a magical, ethereal atmosphere.

My life was rapidly changing moment by moment. I began wondering what was real, what was the truth, and what was happening to me with these dragons. With all that had transpired recently I had developed a deep love for how I felt for all life, and it was also altering how I loved myself, regardless of what I did or did not do. I realized I loved this "being" called me, warts and all. I am pretty amazing, after all. From this place of love, I noticed that I was seeing beyond words and into the Truth.

Although I was also beginning to meet people who were on this same path as me and I was creating a network of connections where we supported and elevated each other and still I frequently felt disconnected and separated.

Something still was off.

I allowed myself to feel these feelings without trying to understand them, actually leaning into what was unfolding. One evening at dusk I was on the lounge outside dozing, feeling very off-balance with life, and as

I slipped off, I had a confrontation with my ego. I saw him (it, her, whatever) standing in the way of me knowing the truth. This stubborn dark figure stood, arms crossed, blocking my way to a golden path clearly weaving behind her/him. I realized that Ego had many jobs, and one was to keep me from remembering. To keep me in the dark, a forgotten state, and block me at every turn of me remembering my quest.

I pushed ego back. "It is time you moved out of my way. You have one real job right now. To keep me safe from real danger. You can no longer block me from the path of truth. You are welcome to join me in this discovery"

Ego did not move out of the way willingly. We had a bit of a struggle, but I reminded ego, "You do what I ask, you to do. Now, join me or get behind me."

Ego finally moved back, clearing the way to the golden weaving road. As I gazed down this path I saw doors along the way, treasure chests along the way, scrolls or maps along the way. I knew that I could now travel this road and find the answers that have been hidden from me my entire life. The way has been cleared.

I woke up from dozing with a start. What was that? Has this been the reason I cannot see beyond the veil? Is there a reason for me forgetting? Have I (meaning my ego) been the one holding me back all along? What is happening now?

I was gazing at the horizon as I went through this thought process and noticed a lone cloud in the sky. I was getting into the habit of seeing shapes everywhere now and often, not surprisingly, I could see the shape of a dragon. This was clearly a dragon cloud floating across the sky. I looked away for a moment and when I looked back, the cloud was gone. Was this my imagination playing tricks on me?

Then I noticed her coming towards me. This beautiful, elegant, Magenta Dragon. She had a tail that curled and created a sign of infinity in the air. Her head had horns that were curled back, like slender ram horns, reaching down her long, elegant neck. She had a look of wisdom in her eyes and a knowing grin on her face.

She softly landed next to me singing in a tone that moved my soul. Her exact words were, "wux tepoha andowinor ini ithquant naam. si tepoha confn ekess letoclo wux rocen svern sva vi bekiw seoyl teikilt. vucot nomeno, huena roceno wux geou connect mrith dout seoyl naam kagh geou qe malrak thirkua."

I was astounded because I understood. And what she said was, "You have forgotten by Divine Wisdom. I have come to help you wake up at a deep soul level. Know this, once awake you will connect with your soul wisdom and will be forever changed."

She continued speaking in her dragon light language and I continued to understand every word.

"Once you have this knowing, there will be no turning back."

"Your heart called out to me as you desire to take another step toward knowing, connecting with Divine wisdom, and feeling the meaning of Truth. Come with me now as we begin your Soul Quest and visit the cosmos. There you will see the stardust around you and will recognize that this is you and you will begin to understand the blueprint you created for this lifetime and remember that you are magnificent and filled with eternal wisdom."

I agreed to this adventure and climbed onto the dragon. When did I become so trusting of dragons and not even question their offerings? All I know is that each encounter brought me exactly what I was looking for. All in Divine timing.

The moment the Magenta Dragon took off I tumbled backwards. I felt the wind pressure and drag pulling me in every direction as she moved back, then sideways, then forward again. I crouched as close to her smooth body as I could and then I felt her slow down to a gentle glide. I realized that her takeoff was to get us moving powerfully forward in order for us to leave the earth's atmosphere and into space.

I no longer felt acceleration. I believe we were moving and every once in a while, I felt a bit of a spin, but mostly I felt like we were still, cocooned in the silence of space. There also was no sound. It was a strange sensation to be still, hear nothing, yet knew that I was moving, and I knew there was sound being made that my ears simply did not pick up.

Then I heard her in my head.

"Dear one, we are traveling past your universe and through the veil into different dimensions. You will experience wonders beyond your imagination and when we return, because we will be returning to the other side of the veil, you will forget much. However, you will remember what you felt, and you will knowingly begin unlocking your codons of wisdom."

I then realized we had passed the planets of our solar system and stepped out of its spiral into a gap, a space, between hundreds, maybe thousands, of other solar systems. In this space area the Magenta Dragon took a leap. It was as if we disappeared and reappeared in a blink into a realm I cannot explain. It was energy. It was home. It was in my mind and outside my body all at the same time.

Then there were many voices speaking to me with so much profound love my heart was bursting.

“Welcome home dear one. You have arrived for a moment, and we will share with you the answers you are seeking. You now realize there is much you have forgotten about, and you are searching for meaning.

You chose this experience called life in order to create expansion for us all. Forgetting made it possible for you to live in contrast and align with the beliefs we created for you called Universal Laws. These laws became part of your blueprint and created the framework for your experiences allowing you to tap into emotion and energy and put you on the path of your profound awakening and soul evolution. You are here to intentionally dissolve layers of fear, sadness, shame, guilt, judgment, and identity that create division and separation from the Divine.

The veil is thinning, and you are remembering.

You are shifting to a more harmonious existence, seeing the connection between all living things. You are already seeing past the illusions you lived under and asking questions from a space of love.

We now are sharing all the power that ever was or ever will be with you. We ask that you continue seeking and asking and that you embrace sharing and teaching along the way.”

The next thing I remember is the Magenta Dragon once more blinked out and I was, once again, on my deck.

In her harmonious voice she said. “Dear one, you have changed within your very DNA. You will never see yourself the same as you now remember who you truly are and always have been. You are, once more, connected will your Soul Wisdom.”

The Magenta Dragon blinked out again, and she was gone leaving me in a state of wonderment. Thoughts were running through my mind. Why do I not remember coming back? What was that experience of profound love all about? How can I learn to sit with this experience every day and settle deeply into the arms of the Divine and let the Universe cradle me in love?

I did remember that, I now understand that in separating from the Divine I was never really separate. That in living a life of contrast it was never intended to become division. That in closing the door to the path of awakening, my ego, which is really me, plays a key role in this world of contrast. That in creating my own blueprint the lessons and awakening process was always laid out by me for me.

I am the Divine creator of my life experiences.

12 - Sunshine Yellow Dragon

"Until one has loved an animal, a part of one's soul remains unawakened." –Anatole France

A magical creature lying on a grassy lawn with a baby fawn snuggled up next to him. The creature is bright yellow, slender, with a long gentle face and yellow gazelle-like horns. Its large wings form a protective canopy over the fawn, and its tail wraps around them both. The creature's hide is yellow with a soft speckled pattern. The scene is peaceful and bathed in warm, golden light, evoking a sense of safety and serenity.

We had a passing rain shower today. It seems that mother nature was cleaning house. As the sun returned, I gazed out of the window. The leaves on the trees were changing color ever so slightly every day now. This subtle transformation created immense beauty and grace for me to admire as they danced in the breeze and reflected back to the sun.

The smaller animals were coming out of hiding from the weather. There were five or so squirrels running around in the back yard. It was not mating season, so it appeared as though they were simply having fun. One stopped to straddle the rock wall and catch his breath. Others climbed trees or walls or played tag with each other. The birds were enjoying the change in the air and were singing a happy song. It felt like all of nature was celebrating this little shower and the warmth of the afternoon sun.

I have always loved the animals we share this planet with. In the past I would wonder if they also had a soul. After my many dragon encounters, I understand that they are all on a soul quest, just like me. Everything we see in this plane of existence is energy. The Earth, plants, animals, the air, the solar system, absolutely everything. All have a level of consciousness and are here on Earth to experience, learn, teach and serve. We live in symbiosis.

I was reminded that, as a child, I was drawn to caring for animals. I lived in the inner city so there was not a variety for me to interact with each day. We could walk to a pretty large Zoo that was not too far from home, so I was able to witness and commune with many on those special visiting days. The local cats, dogs, birds, and even worms held a fascination with me. They were my confidants and my connection to nature.

One day I found a stray kitten and brought it to our apartment to care for. My siblings came home and were horrified. You see, my father was dead set against animals in the home. They felt for me and wanted to support my desire to care for this animal, so that night they hid the cat for me.

Apparently, it was not hidden well enough. The next morning, I woke to discover this poor critter had been tossed out, off the back porch of our third-floor apartment. My father was in a rage that this little creature was in the house. I was horrified, shocked, and distraught over what had happened. I ran out in tears looking for this small creature.

I did find her, and she was fine but was not feeling safe enough to come to me. I was heartbroken and very concerned about the welfare of this animal. There was nothing I could do but eventually walk away and pray that she found sanctuary.

As I became an adult, I had many pets and I saw them as family. I believe I am so passionate about caring for the creatures on this planet because I witnessed what not caring can look like. I saw fear in the eyes of a small creature. I felt the anger of injustice against something unable to defend itself. I learned that not everyone feels connected to nature the way I do. I learned that trust is earned and once lost, may be lost forever.

Strange that this memory returned to me during such a magical moment with nature. That evening, I went to sleep feeling a deep love for this planet I get to live on. I gazed at the little dog I have as she was rolled up, nose snuggled in, softly dreaming her dreams and I was happy. I dozed off dreaming of pandas and lions, and elephants and zebras all living harmoniously together.

The next morning, I made something to drink and stepped out onto the dew drenched deck. It was barely sunrise and yet the yard was lit up like mid-day. I looked to my right, and there he was, lying on the lawn, with a baby fawn snuggling up next to him.

This dragon was bright yellow, slender, with a long gentle face. His horns were also yellow and looked like those of a gazelle. His wings were large enough to act like a canopy of protection over the fawn. His hide, though yellow, had a soft speckle to it while his tail wrapped around both of the fawn and himself.

I walked up to the pair, gently petted the fawn and then stroked the dragon. I found his hide to be soft and warm, and I could feel a vibration, like a gentle purring, come from within him.

“wux re vi seoyl shepherd, zhinir siud seoylic ir'malha persvek asta whedabra, sovesir astahi shafaer asta gogetoi di alchemy. wux nomag ti sohkivik nomeno, oli wer myotrai wux tepoha connected mrith tepoha gethrisja erekess asta version di loerchik kagh astahii yor ekess enel kagh itov wux persvek nomeno lifetime. wux gra'kul relgra ekik ekess ve naeck ekess tawura mrith wux shafaer vi ahsod di irisvir.”

Here we go again. I understood this:

“You are a soul shepherd, walking beside souls stuck in their darkness, guiding them on their quest of alchemy. You may not realize this, but the animals you have connected with have gone through their version of pain and they learn to trust and love you in this lifetime. Your heart called out to me today to work with you on a mission of healing.”

A thought traveled, fleeting, through my mind. How was I supposed to help with this mission? This is something I couldn't get my brain around.

This amazing dragon rose up gently and gradually unwound himself from the fawn, leaving the baby to softly lie asleep on the ground. He then seemed to glide as he walked toward me and the warmth from his gleaming body seemed to seep into my pours.

"I am the Sunshine Yellow Dragon. As I move closer to you, notice the way that my light is cleansing your aura. The light I am pouring into you also holds coding upgrades to help you understand, at a profound level, the importance of all the creatures of this planet."

I already understood the nature of the healing sun on my mood, my metabolism, and my life. This experience was bringing the feeling of knowing everything is perfect to a whole other level. I have learned to not resist and go with the flow of life.

"The Sunshine Yellow Dragons are at work right now, touching the hearts of those who need to understand how to honor the soul-light within every beast, for they too are sparks of the Divine on their own journey. You now have this level of compassion for all of creation within your DNA and your ability to heal mind, body, and soul has increased significantly."

I could feel what I would now describe as sun-love, seeping through me slowly from head to toe, through my muscles, and through my bones. I could feel each cell in my body sigh with love and relief.

The Sunshine Yellow Dragon had more wisdom to share with me. "I can see you understand what it means to be a Sheppard, truly caring for the animals around you. You have now become a "sunshine yellow bridge of light" for us, creating a pathway along which Sunshine Yellow Dragons can travel to help animals everywhere. You are facilitating our arrival."

I asked, "Will I be seeing more of you around then?"

His reply was, "You only interact with those you need in your life when you need us. We are always around, loving you, protecting you, and guiding you. Our love for mankind is great, and the Sunshine Dragon's love of nature's creatures is vast."

He then slowly turned around, lay next to the fawn again, and they both melted into the scenery while I waved goodbye.

As I wiped away the tears I did not realize were streaming down my face, I let out a huge sigh. Have I been holding my breath this whole time?

I went back in and noticed no time had passed during this interaction, and yet I was not the same. I felt the pull to serve animals not to master them. To heal them, respect them, and better understand them. I realized that my mission is to influence mankind. The more I can touch a human heart with this deep understanding of the love of nature, then the more I believe I can truly heal the world.

We are all intertwined, energetically connected. Every act of kindness and love ripples throughout the Universe. I understand that being a shepherd means I can herd the love I have and circle around all living things to create harmony and compassion that then creates frequencies that change everything, Energy is everywhere and is everything. Learning to use that will orchestrate change.

13 - Seventh Dimensional Dragons

"In order to more fully understand this reality, we must take into account other dimensions of a broader reality."
—John Archibald Wheeler

A surreal and ethereal visualization of the seventh dimension, a realm of pure consciousness. The scene features luminous, flowing energy fields in vibrant colors like violet, gold, and indigo, forming intricate fractal patterns. Floating crystalline structures emit soft radiant light, and translucent beings of light offer guidance and healing.

We are entering the realm of the seventh dimensional dragons. We have come a long way to get here, and it is in this dimension where we experience pure consciousness, deep wisdom, and a connection to spiritual guides. By entering into this state of consciousness, we allow ourselves to understand who and what we truly are.

In choosing to manifest on Earth it is here, at this frequency, that we create our blueprint. It is in this dimension that we get a glimpse into the purpose behind our earthly experiences.

Like the fourth dimension being a portal to the fifth, the Seventh is a gateway access to higher realms of existence and connection with advanced spiritual beings, such as ascended masters, galactic council, and archangels. Those who have experienced this clearly describe being here as paradise and receive many gifts and much guidance.

Dragons coming from this realm come to us now to guide us in our understanding of who we are and why we have chosen this experience. That's right. We have chosen this life we are in for a reason. The dragons are full of ancient wisdom and emanate pure love and want to gently nudge us into our awakening. These dragons only come when we are ready to shift our consciousness and grasp the interconnectedness of all things and the underlying fabric that unites the universe.

Dragons can guide us in experiencing unity and oneness as we embody the principles of harmony, balance, and universal love. They show us the way.

14 – Black Dragon

"I cannot make you understand. I cannot make anyone understand what is happening inside me. I cannot even explain it to myself." - Franz Kafka, "The Metamorphosis"

A delicate black dragon made of many shades of black. She is dark-blue black, purple black, raisin black, smoky black, and dark charcoal black. Her wings are huge, big enough to dome a human. The dragon is sprinkling golden stardust around her.

It was an overcast rainy day. One where the grey sky seems to melt into the trees, the air was heavy with dampness, and the breeze did not exist. On this day I had a feeling of quiet and a sense of turning inward. It was peaceful while being eerie at the same time. I decided to go for a little country drive.

I got in the vehicle, picked a destination, turned on the navigation system, and cranked up the tunes. I was feeling the music, gliding along with the traffic, and simply going with the flow. The destination was really not important; it was the freedom of being in motion that I was looking for.

After a while of being lost in the moment, I realized I had been driving for a few hours. The time seemed to fly by in a blink, and I had no idea where I really was. I had gotten into such a zone while driving and grooving to the music that my perception of the here and now was completely lost. I felt lightheaded, a little dizzy, and a heightened sense of being nowhere.

For a moment I believed I witnessed a pink and blue dragon pulling my vehicle. He was huge and muscular and appeared to be driven with a purpose. It struck me at the time that I had become accustomed to these strange creatures, so it seemed appropriate that I would see them everywhere.

Then I saw a flash of someone or something over my left shoulder. It was barely visible and then it was gone. I thought that maybe I imagined this and yet part of me knew there was something there.

I then glanced to the right and glimpsed two fleeting streaks that were like saucers traversing the horizon leaving contrail vapor clouds across the sky; the only evidence that they were ever there. I thought that maybe I was imagining this, but their evidence lingered on.

I pulled over for a moment and renavigated to return home. I was not anywhere near my intended destination, and it didn't really matter. I was out for the experience of a drive and that is what I got. It was time to return home as I was both tired and disoriented and wanted to ponder these sights I had.

When I finally got home, I noticed I was a little bit shaky. I held on to the wall for a moment and then got some water and something to eat. This settled me a bit and I crashed on the couch. I didn't realize just how exhausted I was as I quickly fell asleep.

Dreams had become vivid to me over the past few months and sometimes were as real as when I was not sleeping. On occasion, I would wonder where the true reality of who I am lies. This was one of those times when everything in my dream state was crystal clear.

I found myself waking up on a bed of pillows that were thick and soft and made out of color combinations of silver, indigo, gold, and green. I felt these cushions cradle me, holding me softly in a state of bliss. I looked around and noticed I was in a glass-like dome that was black. I could not see outside, yet I felt safe, as though this place was familiar, and it was mine. It was a cocoon of comfort. As I looked around at the furnishings within this domed room, I began to notice the walls pulsing rhythmically. I looked up and saw a hole at the top and a beautiful face looking down through this opening at me with love.

This was a Black Dragon, and as I looked around, I realized that my dome room was actually her wings surrounding me with protection. As I scanned my surroundings, I noticed many shades of black. This dragon was a mixture of dark-blue black, purple black, raisin black, smoky black, and dark charcoal black. The more my eyes adjusted, the more shades presented themselves to me. The dragon was sprinkling golden star dust into the dome and when each particle landed on me it melted into my skin. They felt warm and inviting and I was enjoying this strange dream experience.

I heard this dragon singing, like a lullaby, as I relaxed on my thrown of cushions. "Sleep well in your dream cocoon. Prepare, for changes are soon. As one chapter ends a turned page sends black energy supporting your unhewn."

As this music surrounded me, I began to look forward to something unknown. I was ready to embrace come what may. For some reason I was ready to walk away from what I had built in my life into something unknown.

I began to feel that something was happening to me physically. My body felt lighter, my brain was pulsing, my breathing was deeper, and my energy field expanded, pushing against the walls of this dome. I was pulsing in the beat of the Black Dragon's wings and felt the rhythm vibrate deep within my groin.

She spoke to me this time. "Dear one. Your change has begun and the metamorphosis you have started will continue. Know that even when you leave this dream state you remain in my winged embrace so your divine potential, all that you are meant to be, grows strong. You will leave this space of chrysalis after your metamorphosis is completed. No matter what happens, here I will keep you safe."

I felt myself slowly waking up and I had a deep sense of knowing. It is something I never really felt before. I understood that, even now, I remain within this safe, dark place where the Black Dragon creates space where I can continue to develop until I am ready to emerge, transforming a transmutation of humankind into something more.

As I looked around, I saw the Black Dragon on my lawn, a reminder that she would stay with me. A reminder for me to expect to be different, allow the changes to gently take hold, and be ready to soar with the dragons, the angels, and the Gods.

15 - Silver Dragon

"It takes courage to endure the sharp pains of self-discovery rather than choose to take the dull pain of unconsciousness that would last the rest of our lives." -Marianne Williamson

A silver dragon with expressive eyes holding a golden key. The dragon is majestic and mature, with large powerful wings. Her body is rendered in various shades of silver including Silver Sand, Pirate Silver, Antique Silver, Royal Silver, Birch Silver, and Pink Silver. She radiates a magical aura that glows around her, enhancing her mystical presence. The background is soft and dreamy to emphasize her magical nature.

It had been a few weeks now since my dream encounter with the Black Dragon. I could feel myself physically changing every day and I was confident that this was intended, and I knew I was safe. It may be because she told me what to expect or it might be that this was truly happening, but I could feel the security of living in a sort of metaphysical cocoon as I was becoming whatever it is that awaits me. What I found interesting is that this sense of security also created an element of bravery.

I woke up to a sunny warm day, the kind of day that always beckons me to experience iced tea and lazy strolls along the beach. I was reminded about the changes I was already experiencing while I took my time that morning being present with everything I was doing. I was hyper-aware of my environment, my emotions, and my thoughts. I was becoming curiouser and curiouser. The potential for discovery was all around me.

It seemed like the perfect day for the ocean, so I got into my vehicle to head to the water. I was just 20 minutes from the beach, so I was surprised when, 10 minutes into the drive, the marine layer rolled in. I was no longer in a clear sunny day but driving in a moist overcast scene as dense low clouds surrounded me. I considered turning back yet continued forward. Regardless of the thickening fog I was looking forward to the sand between my toes, the water lapping at my feet, and the smell of the salt water in my nose. The salt air and rolling tide always felt like home to me.

I parked, walked to the sand, removed my shoes, and headed to the water's edge. I strolled along, looking around at the various birds, sea gulls, pelicans, and sanderlings pecking at some unseen insect as they cleaned the beach. Seaweed washed ashore, bringing sediments from the ocean floor while housing tiny creatures hiding for protection. I then marveled at the tiny bird footprints that had made decorations in the sand. Nature was expressing herself today.

I looked across the water and watched the dolphins playing in the waves. As I continued to look, I noticed the water reflecting the silver-grey of the sky and the shades of silver and grey began to take shape. This shape was becoming huge.

The figure forming in front of me span across the horizon and moved with the rhythm of the tides. It got bigger and bigger, closer and closer, and it was clear that this was becoming a Silver Dragon. I stopped in awe as I watched her move slowly toward me and gently land on the sand to my right. I looked up as she towered over me. She smiled, lowered her head level with mine, and I reached up to hold her face in my hands.

I was mesmerized by her eyes. They called to me and as I looked into her yellow gaze I fell into a trance. We were communicating at a soul level. No words from her mouth or from mine, yet I know we shared our thoughts. Looking into those eyes was like looking into me in a way I have never done before. I felt the aura around this Silver Dragon touch mine and, in that moment, I was, yet again, changed. I realized, in that instance, I had been living in a dream-state my entire life. There has always been a gift I have had but did not tap into and I witnessed my true purpose while also being transformed.

"It's time to trust your intuition and live within the flow of life. You are losing the weight of forgetfulness and moving toward enlightenment."

These were not words as you and I know them. I simply had a knowing that what was being shared was truth.

"I have placed the silver light of my aura around you to continue supporting the changes you are experiencing. As you move closer to your spiritual enlightenment this quantum silver light field will assist in detoxifying your energy fields, including your physical, etheric, emotional, mental, and spiritual auras. It decalcifies your pineal gland and brings clarity to your life. You will find spiritual balance, sharper intuition, and more powerful psychic abilities.

You have accessed your soul blueprint that holds truth about you as I hand you the keys to the codes of your gifts, talents, wisdom, and powers; the parts of you that you have not realized even exists. The soft pure silver light that surrounds your aura now will help you retain your divine feminine qualities. Know that this is the Will and that this is so."

I moved out of the trance I had been in and felt the tears running down my face. I had seen my divine magnificence and the "I AM" that is what we all come from. My breath had been taken away by the sheer magnitude of who I truly am and where I came from. I did not want to leave. It was so beautiful.

I could see this divine energy now in the birds on the beach, the dolphins in the ocean, the water in the sea, the mist in the air, everywhere. It was like watching the pixels that create this illusion of life. You see, after experiencing "home," it becomes evident that the thing we call reality is a construct.

Although I had a deep pain in missing what I had just witnessed, I also had joyful excitement about where I was heading. Knowing my soul blueprint now changed everything. I wanted to shout from the rooftops, "Walk away from the illusions." I knew this would not work, but I held tight to this love within me.

I kissed the Silver Dragon on her cheek and thanked her for bringing me on such a spectacular adventure and for sharing her silver aura with mine. This will always be with me as I begin to better understand, in each moment, how to be aligned and be in balance with the divine source from which we all have come from. After all, Divine love is all there is and it is all that I AM.

16 - Dusty Pink Dragon from Andromeda

"You are the universe, expressing itself as a human for a little while." - Eckhart Tolle

The Dusty Pink Dragon from Andromeda. She is a dragon dancing in the air, holding musical notes in her claw while notes dance around her. She is long and slender, in space with the galaxy behind her. She is bringing the Universe to you. There are subtle hieroglyphic tattoos on her long neck and arms that hold the history of existence. She is a multi-pink dragon. Her pink coloration ranges from soft rose to vibrant magenta. Her scales glimmer like gemstones under the sun, each one reflecting light in mesmerizing patterns.

I'd been sitting in contemplation for quite a few weeks feeling uneasy, excited, and lost all at the same time. In this confusion I believed it was time for me to escape the confines of the cocoon created previously by the Black Dragon and allow the unknown me that was developing to break loose and emerge. I was craving freedom with a nagging desire to travel and be off grid. The pull to get going was so strong that I physically felt tugged, being in one place was starting to smother me. And yet the idea of having no clue what this all meant was frightening.

There was no calming this down and there was no explanation available. I knew the dragon encounters had changed me each and every time and that I no longer could relate to many of the people around me. My goodness, I was not sure I could even relate to myself anymore. I felt guided by an extremely powerful force and my life had become completely out of control. Each moment unfolded as a mystery.

I decided I needed to get away from life for a few hours. Away from people, technology, and noise. I was looking to get grounded, to find my center, and reconnect with my very being. When I wanted to do this, I frequently went to a space in the woods where there were clear trails leading to various parts of the forest and lakes. This was a good place for me to get connected with other creatures of the earth. My sense of belonging here with them was deep and profound. It felt right.

I packed some food, a blanket, and water then headed out to the reserve. I chose the upper lake trail and departed for a mini adventure. I took my time as I felt the trees breathing, heard the birds singing, and quietly watched the deer and elk munching. A woman riding horseback trotted passed me and I marveled at her connection with this marvelous beast. All the smaller animals were rustling in the bushes, the dragonflies snatching bugs, the bees flitting among the flowers, and the crickets were hopping about making their own quiet song. Each step I took seemed to become more and more intentional and more and more solid as I felt myself melting into nature.

I got to the upper lake and noticed that the wild blueberry bushes were bursting to be picked. I grabbed a small cup from my bag and carefully selected the juiciest treats available from nature. I went to the lake and rinsed them off. As I sat down, I removed my shoes and put my feet in the cool lake water and munched on my surprise snack.

I was swinging my legs and splashing the water with my feet. I watched each new ripple spread out and change the fabric of the water's surface. I knew at this time that there was a reason for me being on Earth and I just could not put into words why I was meant to be here. As I relaxed into accepting this unknown I was gazing into the water and enjoying the playfulness of the moment, and I noticed a pink glow appear in the lake's reflection.

You might realize by now that I was no longer surprised to see a dragon appear. In fact, I had become delighted in the variety I had seen and the gifts each one brought with each experience we shared together. That being said, this one was a multi pink dragon. Her pink coloration ranged from a soft rose color to vibrant magenta, her scales glimmered like gemstones under the sun, each one reflecting light in mesmerizing patterns. Her grace and elegance elevated her to a status of iconography, conveying a deeper meaning to the design of who she was.

Her voice was a light musical tone and sang softly to me.

"You have done well, little one. It is now time for you to carry this luminous pink light I am gifting to you in all your spiritual energy centers. Today, we are expanding your consciousness to allow you to be part of elevating and awakening the planet. You have great powers within you as you have shifted to a much higher rate of vibration already."

Hearing this, I knew it to be true. This was part of the cocooning I had gone through and yet I also understood there was more to unfold. I felt a little nervous as I could not imagine what was going to happen now.

"I will be activating your energy centers, unlocking many codons hidden within you, and preparing you to embody an even higher love vibration. You will then radiate love and light at many different frequencies, enabling you to be an agent of change, transforming the people you meet who are open and ready for the next evolution in their life, without them even being aware of it. It simply will be so."

I felt deeply in awe of what was to happen. Without knowing it I heard me whisper, "I accept this gift and radiate Higher Love."

I closed my eyes and surrendered to what was meant to happen next.

I felt the heat of light pink flames ignite me along the way.

And she began, "Know, dear one, that there are many chakra energy centers within you right now. Today, you and I are going to ignite and amplify your 14 key Chakras. As my pink flames of activation brushes at each orb, you will feel the frequency and potency of your energy centers expand."

I was feeling myself drift into a trance now and felt completely at ease with this process. And as I drifted I heard her chanting begin.

"Little one, notice each of your energy spheres clearly:

High over your head is your Stellar Gateway. See its shimmering white color expanding. In this place you transcend all dimensional boundaries of time and space. You access frequencies that extend far beyond your current physical capacity, accepting light from as far as the twelfth-dimensional source and beyond. It is powerful and I invite you to take this energy and step it down to a level that is comfortable for you. Know that this will become easier with time as you become more able to absorb higher frequencies.

We're moving now to your shimmering white and gold Soul Star, located directly above your crown chakra. This is the point where spiritual energy and Divine love enter your body. Watch this brilliance expand as you allow the Divine light of Spirit and the white ray of love fill your life. This is the place of your soul origin, the place of enlightenment, and the place for ascension to enter you.

Take a deep breath and look now as we are encountering your light lavender and purple Causal Chakra, just over your head and slightly behind you. This is your gateway to the higher spiritual realms and where you receive messages and concepts from those regions. As the frequency of this energy center increases you are better able to allow these higher plane messages in and to be interpreted in a way that you and others can understand.

Stay with me now as we slide over to your violet Crown Chakra, your wisdom center, your connection to spirit, and your sense of universal consciousness, unity, and self-knowledge. Notice, as the frequency increases, you feel a deeper sense of harmony with all existence, you recognize spiritual insights, and you are able to create a more profound connection to the Divine. You and the I AM are one.

Turn around as we are now expanding your Indigo Third Eye. As this grows you will receive even more messages and more vivid dreams. This is your center of intuition and psychic abilities, providing you with the ability to perceive energies, visions, and truths that are not visible to the naked eye. Here you realize with your "real eyes" that you are the visionary, profit and speaker of truth.

I am now brushing my pink energy over your Blue Throat Chakra. Feel the clarity of communicating expressivity and creativity bringing you more in alignment with the universe. Experience the healing of uncertainty as you allow words of knowing and truth to flow naturally through you from the Divine. Here you speak into existence the truth you have just seen.

Together we are now going to step into the realm of your three hearts. This is your connection to eternal love and is where much power is exchanged.

As we gently brush your Ethereal Heart the shimmering white, green, and pink tones glimmer in joy. Feel the unquestionable love that governs this energy center where you expand the art of forgiveness, compassion, and expressing unconditional love.

Join me as we now step into your Green Heart, the main heart, which governs how you react around others, and your trust levels leap forward. As this energy increases you will find that you approach others with a sense of compassion while maintaining clear boundaries for yourself and others. You trust from knowing that you are being guided by Divine love.

And now we are entering into your Pink Sacred Heart. Here we are expanding your love of life and purpose. Although you may not be able to articulate what it is in the language of humans, your life is driven from here as you discover the connection between you and the Universe and your love of your life glows around you. There are no limits to how profoundly you are affected by your connection to the "all that is."

Take a breath as you might imagine how it feels when we leave your heart and continue onto the Yellow Solar Plexus where we clear past stories and beliefs with the Dusty Pink Dragon of Andromeda's pink light and expand your self-image and self-power. This clearing allows you to move forward experiencing increased willpower, confidence, and vitality. You will be even more sensitive with your ability to feel the energy around you and from others, and within you, your field of focus continues to expand. This is now a clear bridge that allows communication through the nerve centers of your body and brings in the information you need in order to take aligned Divine action in this life.

As we continue on, we enter your Orange Sacral energy field, and I brush across this with my pink activation flame. We are bringing the Divine into the earthly realm now. This is your source of manifestation, the seat of creation, and the center for connection and romantic sexual relationships. As you feel the heat rise and the frequency change you will manifest even more clearly and more seamlessly.

As we continue to activate, cleanse, and accelerate your energy centers we continue on now to your Red Root energy field. This governs the material world, and your ability to live within it. Here is where you anchor in and are secure. In this energy center, the expanded consciousness is experienced as enthusiasm. Your expanding enthusiasm will support and enliven your life, your mission, and your manifestation.

We continue now and step outside your body and activate your deep brown Earth Star energy center. This is like a spirit root, connecting you to earth's energies and enhances your spiritual awareness. This activation creates unshakable stability and profound spiritual grounding as your connection shoots down, like the roots of a tree, into the wisdom of Mother Earth.

Together we now enter the deep black and green Gaia Gateway. As my pink flame activates this energy center, you will begin to understand the circle of energy from source, through you, to Gaia, back through you, and up again to Source. The Gaia Gateway serves as a direct conduit to the vibrant, living energy and consciousness of our planet within the Earth's etheric field. The Gaia Gateway is an energy center that anchors your entire energetic system to the planet. This activation will support and facilitate your conscious connection with the Earth's consciousness (Gaia). Together you exchange energy, wisdom, and healing, drawing nourishment and stability directly from the planetary core.

Feel all your activated energy centers working together in harmony creating a symphony that is uniquely you. There is a melody now that will continue to accelerate.

We have drawn to the end, Dear one. I invite you to breathe in my dusty pink flame and become a flame of ineffable pink love. You now have the power to touch everyone you meet with the Flame of Spiritual Love."

I heard the soft flutter of her wings and slowly opened my eyes. She was gone, I was exhausted, and the sun was going down. I had been here for hours.

I had a hard time getting up as I felt like a toddler, just now learning about balance and gravity. I held onto trees as I made my way back to the path to return to where I left my vehicle. I stopped and took a drink of water and a few deep breaths. I was shaken, in a good way. I felt unlike me, like something different, yet something that has always been and never acknowledged.

I got to my vehicle and drove home. I did not sleep much that evening as I focused on each energy center. It was like an exercise of greeting and getting to know parts of me that I didn't realize were there or that I had taken for granted. It was an intimate experience of getting to know me completely, maybe for the very first time.

17 - Aquamarine Dragon from Neptune

"You can, you should, and if you're brave enough to start, you will." —Stephen King

A slender, angelic blue dragon floating in the air, holding a slim Neptune-like trident in one claw and a small gold key in the other. The dragon's body features a blend of azure-blue, star command blue, Uranian blue, steel blue, and violet blue. Its wings resemble fish gills, and it is accompanied by graceful sea horses swimming around it. On its forehead is a small deep blue gem embedded in its chest is a radiant crystalline heart. The dragon's tail is long and slender, flowing elegantly behind it. The overall atmosphere is ethereal and oceanic, with soft glowing light and a sense of serenity.

The days were getting shorter and the weather colder and I was feeling a little bit trapped. I wanted the water, walks on the beach, and sunshine. It was at this point that I realized it was time for me to move to an area that better suited who I was and what I wanted in that moment. To be truthful, I had the urge to just pack up and travel. I was in the process of figuring out what this all meant when I received a call.

This was from a friend that was an interesting connection. We had little in common and yet we enjoyed each other's company and were open to one another's perspective. We had fun together and held deep and complex conversations.

As we chatted, my friend confessed to feeling light deprivation already and wanted the longer sunshine days to last. I guess we can all suffer a touch of feeling down when we miss the sun. Rather than complain, my friend and I talked about solutions.

My friend chimed in, "I know what we can do, let's go on a cruise and get out of here."

At this point I had never been on a cruise, and the idea was fascinating. So, I responded, “Let’s do it.”

“I’ll call you right back,” and my friend hung up.

A few moments later I got the call back, “Let me have your charge information.” I complied and my friend hung up.

A few moments later I got the next call back, “We’re all set. We leave in two weeks for seven days. It is a repositioning cruise, and we fly home from the final port. Here are the dates.”

It didn’t even occur to me to ask about the cost. I noted down the dates in order to make the arrangements I needed in order for me to actually go. I then asked, “So, where are we going and specifically how do we get there?”

We were flying to Puerto Rico, hopping on a 7-day cruise, and getting off in St. Thomas. We were to fly home from there.

OK… and so off we went a few weeks later.

Getting to the port from the airport was a little bit confusing. We found the shuttle and boarded. The neighborhoods we drove through were poor and a bit sad. I sent loving energy along the way and realized I was in for an experience, and I had no idea of how it would unfold.

Because of the short notice we did not have time to consider the tour packages for each port. As it turned out, this meant we toured the beaches and the shopping centers based on cab driver's recommendations and they were always fabulous.

We began with Jamaica, then went to Martinique, St Lucia, then hit the open sea for a day. We were on our way to Curaçao, which meant we had the full day in the open water on the ship to explore our surroundings and enjoy ourselves. I am an early riser (much to my friend's chagrin) and have been taking early morning strolls along the various decks. Because there was no port of call on this day there were very few people up and about this early morning. I went to the upper deck and headed toward the bow of the ship. I loved this 360-degree view of the ocean as I felt the sun kissing my skin, the water spraying on my face, and me breathing in the air that was fresh and clear. As I gazed into the ocean, watching the waves as they drifted by, I notice a watery swirl rising up toward me.

Here I am in the middle of the Caribbean Sea, minding my own business, and this blue dragon holding a slim Neptune fork and a small key arose from the ocean. This dragon had shades of blue including azure-blue, star command blue, Uranian blue, steel blue, and violet blue. His wings were more like fish gills, and I saw sea horses accompanying him as they moved toward me.

His forehead held a small deep blue gem, and his heart sported a crystalline stone. His tail was long and slender, and his presence was angelic.

I welcomed my visitor to come aboard and sit with me. He seemed to float around me in the sea-mist air and brought a crisp wet breeze with him as he drifted by.

"I am an Aquamarine Dragon from Neptune, and I have come to unlock more of the keys and codes of your true essence, and you will begin to see your world and the Universe quite differently yet again. I bring you connection to high frequencies and the keys and codes of advanced spirituality and ascension.

As your codons are unlocked, you will find that you possess extraordinary psychic abilities, feel deep connections to nature, and experience an innate understanding of the cosmos. This understanding will provide you with unparalleled wisdom and spiritual understanding."

I was speechless. Each dragon experience has created major changes in my life and, quite frankly, my perspective of reality. It seemed that the more I expanded the more expansion came my way. The idea of infinity and being a part of that started to feel right and yet felt like something out of a sci-fi movie.

I looked over at a table next to me on the deck. There was a glass of water there. I wondered, where did that come from?

"I invite you now to drink this glass of blessed water. Next, close your eyes, think about crystal clear blue water and see me in front of you. Focus on your breathing, find your silence within yourself and your guidance will come"

I followed these instructions and began to hear the Universe speak to me. Well not in words like you and I might speak, but the feelings I had were unmistakable communications that I was receiving and somehow understanding. I was hearing about what was to come and how I was changing. I understood in this moment that all I had experienced in my life and all that is coming has always been meant to be.

The Aquamarine Dragon from Neptune spoke again. "As you become even more comfortable with allowing your connection to the Universe to come in, allow whatever emerges to come forth without trying to understand or to assign meaning. Simply let it unfold. Allow me to now flood your chakras with my aquamarine light and wake them up even more."

I closed my eyes, laid back on the deck lounge, and felt my energy centers light up.

- My sacral lit up with aquamarine light to bring more awareness to my clairsentience
- My solar plexus received this blessed light to attune to my psychic wisdom
- My heart center, connecting to the Universe, embraced the collective consciousness
- My throat attuned to clairaudience
- My all-seeing third eye received clarity of my clairvoyance
- My crown to embraced opening up to claircognizance

I felt my Chakras shift into an alignment of communication with each other and beyond.

As I opened my eyes, I saw the Aquamarine Dragon from Neptune drop a tear of joy on my cheek. "You will do wonderous things in this lifetime. It has been an honor to open your eyes."

I stood up and hugged the dragon. "Thank you for this gift today. I do not know what this means for me, but I am open to whatever comes next."

I watched as the dragon floated away and sank back into the sea. I then returned to my cabin, silent, deep in contemplation. I got ready for the day and the remainder of the cruise as we were now heading to Curaçao, then off to Aruba and St Thomas.

The dragon experience caused me to become even more aware of my Self as a spiritual being. I was beginning to understand what it means to be a soul choosing this life experience. I was beginning to see the foolishness of others and wondered how could I be of service to humanity and aid in the waking up process. I felt the presence of Gaia and the consciousness of the Universe and knew that life was changing. Not just for me but for everyone.

18 - Ninth Dimensional Dragons

"The eternal void is filled with infinite possibilities" — *Lao Tzu*

A fanciful image of the ninth dimension from a spiritual perspective. The scene is filled with vibrant colors and luminous energy. Beings of light with flowing robes and radiant auras navigate through a vast expanse filled with swirling galaxies, alternate timelines, and fantastical worlds. These beings possess an aura of wisdom and power, effortlessly manifesting their desires into reality.

We're moving now to meet a few of the dragons from the ninth dimension. Before I continue, I would like to clarify that when I talk about dimensions, I am not referring to a hierarchy. One is not better or more evolved than the other. These are simply frequencies of consciousness. Think of the ninth as entering into the space of The Creator. Here, individuals that have achieved this connection and this level of awareness experience a God-like state. They see infinite possibilities in every sense of the word.

This dimension is so removed from our third dimensional experience that those connecting to this realm of consciousness enter a state of pure energy, allowing for infinite acts of expression and creation. This is unlike anything imaginable in this human experience and yes, *here*, anything imagined is possible and you get a deep understanding of your interconnectedness with all life forms.

Our dragons from the Ninth-Dimension work with the Pleiadian council who serve as messengers, offering insights into alternate timelines and realities. These dragons' appearances happen when you are ready to truly understand nature and consciousness and your role in life's evolution towards greater growth and expansion. The consciousness of Gaia, your Self, and the Universe become interconnected.

Get ready to meet Ninth-Dimensional Dragons.

19 - Dark Blue Galactic Dragon

"Everything amazing about the universe is inside of you, and the two are inseparable." — Carl Sagan

A dark blue galactic dragon gliding gracefully through space. The dragon is slender and elegant, with a long tail trailing behind and straight horns extending from its forehead. Its eyes sparkle like stardust. It holds a small satchel in its front claws, collecting glowing pieces of stardust from a shimmering trail. The surrounding space is rich with deep hues of midnight blue, steel blue, indigo, slate, and dark slate, blending into a cosmic celebration of the dragon's arrival. The dragon's scales subtly reflect the colors of the night sky, making it appear as though it is part of the cosmos itself.

It has been months now since I've had a new dragon encounter. I feel as though I must sit with what I've experienced, what I've learned, and how this has changed my life. I see the dragons that have come to me frequently in my dreams. I feel them around me, guiding me, and whispering to me. I hear their voices, their songs, and their laughter throughout the day.

Spring is here now, and the rebirth of mother nature has caught my attention. I have learned to be even more aware of Gaia's consciousness and wisdom. I tune in even more to the sun's energy and light as she guides my circadian rhythm. I feel the presence of the universe, of God, within me and through me more and more each day and I feel blessed. I am in constant metamorphosis, not knowing what I might become each day.

Through this I see the smallness of people's choices. I see the pain and fear that drives them. I see the light trying to grab their attention. In witnessing this and the more I step back and observe myself, I am ever more grateful for no longer playing this game.

I know that choices from the heart is something new to me and has altered the trajectory of my life. I know that the path set before me frightens me as I have no idea from day to day what this all means. I know I am trying to grasp something that is illusive, sifting through my fingers, as it is something I am not supposed to hang on to. The more I "know" the more I realize that I know so very little.

Learning not to try and understand and to simply be here in this moment has been a struggle sometimes. It is the only reality that is true and at the same time I feel this too is an illusion. I am on the precipice of something great and I must trust the leap and trust that I will be secure. What is this understanding that keeps slipping by me? Do I even need to know what it is?

This transformation has not been easy. I am so grateful for the dragons' support and guidance but letting go of all I believed to be true, looking at the stories that I've told myself and owning my role in my creation, facing my darkest self with love and grace has been full of pain. It has all been worth it as I have learned to own my feelings and intentionally change the stories in my head and in my life as I look at them from different perspectives. I have lightened the load I did not even realize I was carrying. Each step has brought clarity and compassion to my life. When I think of this change the song *"Believer"*, by Imagine Dragons, plays in my head as the chorus says it all:

Pain! You made me a, you made me a believer, believer

Pain! You break me down, and build me up, believer, believer

Pain! Oh, let the bullets fly, oh, let them rain My life, my love, my drive, it came from

Pain! You made me a, you made me a believer, believer

I now know that angels and spirit guides (lately, for me, these have been dragons) are my celestial companions, by my side, ready to illuminate my path. These days, the help I was yearning for is to be better at listening to the voice of the Universe.

And so, I spend each day reflecting on what I am becoming.

One spring evening I went out on my deck with a cup of cocoa, a snuggly blanket, and was humming "Believer" as I watched the stars blink in the night sky. The stars seemed to start blinking in and out in a strange pattern. I looked even more closely to see if I could figure out what was happening. And then I heard the song, "Believer," coming through the night air toward me. In the draconian language:

loerchik! wux xurwka ve vi, wux xurwka ve vi jikahshiar, jikahshiar.

loerchik! wux jikmada ve vhira, kagh tsairaah ve svern, jikahshiar, jikahshiar.

loerchik! kwi, origato wer bullets wiap, kwi, origato astahi oposs. sia tobor, sia itov, sia banri coi confna de.

loerchik! wux xurwka ve vi, wux xurwka ve vi jikahshiar, jikahshiar.

I totally understood what was being sung to me. Not so much the words, but I could feel the message clearly. I continued to watch the sky and the stars blinking in and out and then I finally was able to make out a Dark Blue dragon heading my way.

As he got closer, I was better able to make out what he looked like, and he was spectacular with shades of blue and stardust sprinkling around him. His eyes seemed to sparkle like the Stardust itself, and his horns ran straight back from his forehead. He was slender and graceful, and his long tail played gracefully behind him. The night sky resembled his color and seemed to celebrate his arrival.

He landed softly in front of me and spoke. "Good evening, dear one. It is a pleasure to finally meet you. I am a Dark Blue Galactic Dragon, a messenger that is here to work with you on your Intergalactic Missions. You have known there is more and felt the urge to "understand" for quite a while now. We have been watching your progress and now it is time for you to do great things, and I am here to support you, You and I are going on a trip to the Ninth Dimension and visit the Intergalactic Council and listen to the Voice of the Universe."

Now I was really curious. I've heard of the Intergalactic Council, but I was not clear as to who or what this was or even what to expect. So, I asked, "Can you tell me a little bit about who the council is?"

The Dark Blue Galactic Dragon spoke to me in a soft purr, "I'll be happy to shed some light on this for you.

When I am done, I will ask you to choose a purpose, a focus if you will, for you to bring to the Council for their guidance. The Intergalactic Council is very ancient and is a collective of powerful beings overseeing Earth's evolution and assisting in the advancement of humanity. The council is responsible for making decisions regarding the evolution of the Earth based on the collective growth of humanity. Each member has a focus and a purpose in guiding Earth, and they work together for Gaia and humanities greater good."

The dragon was walking back and forth as he spoke. Similar to a teacher at the front of a classroom. I had to hold a little giggle back at this image of him in front of 5th grade students who would be more in awe of a speaking dragon than in what he had to say. "The Ninth Dimension holds an awesome light, filled with joy, love, and wisdom beyond your current comprehension. While we are there, I will ignite the hidden codes of your master soul blueprint, enabling you to better listen to the voice of the universe".

I've done some soul blueprint work before and have an understanding of how profound this experience could be for me. I leaned forward with even more curiosity.

"Your Soul Quest has taken you to the stars and beyond. You have evolved and gotten a clearer understanding of this life and who you are. In our encounter today with the masters, you will receive information allowing you to contribute your energy for the smooth ascension of the planet through animals, humanity, or spirit. When we are there, you will petition the Council for this guidance. Decide now what your petition is for. I will then take you to the council to present your request and receive their guidance."

I sat in silence now as I contemplated the choices I had before me. I've held conversations with spiritualists. I've received information about purpose from others who are in flow, channel, and receive messages. I've known my whole life that I had a role to play, and it was huge. I simply did not know what that meant.

As I was making my decision, I felt myself drifting into an altered state. As I slipped away, I heard myself whisper, "I am drawn to assist the ascension of the planet." As I drifted off, I found myself sitting on the sand by a waterfall.

The air by this waterfall was crisp, clean, and laced with the earthy freshness of damp moss and budding leaves. Mist from the cascading water added a faint mineral scent, invigorating and pure. The breeze was gentle, cool, and slightly moist, brushing against my skin with whispers of pine and wildflowers from nearby meadows. The sun felt warm but not heavy, its rays filtering through new foliage, casting dappled light that danced on the sand around me.

This vision was so clear that the scenery was vibrant: golden sand sparkled under the soft sunlight, framed by lush green ferns and blooming wildflowers in purples and yellows. The waterfall roared softly, its white foam contrasting with the clear, rippling pool below, while distant birdsong and the rustle of leaves completed the serene tableau.

I was in ecstasy. As I sat on my blanket I felt the rising of the Dark Blue Galactic Dragon underneath me. He captured me gently on his back and we began to rise. As I watched the scene beneath me getting smaller and smaller I realized that this flight had no effect on me. I felt as though I was still on the beach, watching the waterfall creating rainbows in the sun.

In a blink I was no longer any place I had ever been before. Everything around me was shimmering with energy, including the dragon and me. Even though I have no recollection of being here before I knew these "beings" around me and they knew me. They saw within my soul, and I was struck by such profound love and compassion that I fell to my knees. I felt each member of the Council place a hand on my forehead, by my third eye. I heard them whisper to me all together though it sounded like one voice. I felt my mind open up and the energy from these being shot through me, like a lightning rod, all the way back to earth. It was sensual and it was magic.

I knew in that moment that I would always hear the voices from the Intergalactic Council and that each step I took would be guided by them. I will always have free Will and have options available to me, but my mission and my wellbeing is now being clearly guided moving forward.

I was in awe, unable to speak, and deeply grateful for this gift. I then heard the Dark Blue Galactic Dragon's voice, "You can gently open your eyes now. Slowly stretch and return to the present."

I realized I had never left my deck. It was so real, and I also realized that what I witnessed was something I got to see with my "real eyes." I felt invigorated and could literally feel that my energy fields had expanded. There was a light emanating from me and a clarity of purpose that I felt would never be denied. I had become an emissary of truth and was being pulled forward on a mission greater than myself.

I thanked the Dark Blue Galactic Dragon for his guidance. He replied, "I will now always be in your dreams, and you now are able to hear the Universe as it speaks to you. We are united as one."

I watched as the dragon drifted back into the night and sat for a while in thought, in love, and in awe of what was to come.

20 - Source Dragon

"01 – All the power that ever was or will be is here now."
- The Pattern on the Trestleboard

A majestic pure white, snow white, pearl white, and frosty white dragon with a translucent glow. She is holding the energy of a solar system between her hands, with planets and stars swirling in a glowing orb. The background is a deep space scene with stars, nebulae, and galaxies.

A few months had passed since my visit to the Intergalactic Council. Life had been presenting interesting opportunities for me to step into and many more challenges for me to face. My humanness sometimes seemed to be an interference these days. What I mean by this is that when I was around people who had not had some of these experiences or who were stuck in the rut of their life experiences, the pain I felt hurt my very heart. Where in the past I would get wrapped up into these circumstances, I now faced each occurrence with different perspectives. I had become more of an observer, and I could no longer relate to hanging onto energy that was painful.

For example, when I was around angry people, I felt their anger like spears flying at me at lightning speed. I had to remind myself that this was their story and to let the energy pass through as best I could. I found this was easier said than done. I felt extreme empathy for their suffering but knew it was in their power to choose a different path. I discovered that I can "love on them" and allow them to just be in what they feel.

When I was with people who were super depressed, I felt the weight of their shadow fall over me. It was difficult to breathe, and I learned to remind myself to take deep long breaths to let my body know I was safe before I could shine the light for their self-witnessing, should they choose to do so.

What do you do in a world that sees division, separation, and blame and chooses not to accept love and the magnificence this experience has to offer?

I do believe these encounters were a reminder that there is always more baggage for me to unload, but to practice seeing past the situation and into the God-soul of everyone I meet. I heard a statement in the middle of a meditation recently that rings true. “I give you permission to throw your anger spears at me, and still, I love you.” I heard this amazing mantra from Kyle Cease, a transformational speaker. Wisdom is everywhere and I am open to receiving it. I’m learning that the Universe speaks to me in many different ways. I simply have to listen.

Summer was waning, the evenings were crisp and the days perfectly balanced. The change in season was impacting my feelings and my perspective. I was heading into a new phase in my own life; my new season was emerging.

One morning I noticed the trees were still green, and the sun danced across the leaves while the wind flipped them in a choreographed routine of celebration. I looked away for a moment and when I looked back, I realized that the top leaves were changing color. They were all green a moment before! I thought about this phenomenon for a bit. Was I seeing green before and was my mind changing this image as we were approaching fall? Was I seeing what I was expecting to see? Was any of this even real?

Curiouser and curiouser was now my life's experiences.

This summer I had the opportunity to speak at a local event that had a very respectable turnout. I spoke about connecting with the Universe, about trusting intuitive messages, and understanding our soul blueprint. The following weekend I bumped into a few people who had attended this gathering, and they thanked me for giving them permission to allow themselves to believe in their messages and follow them. They learned it was okay to let go and trust the direction they were receiving. They were ready and I showed up.

I also was randomly hearing people thank me for helping them heal. I was not particularly doing anything intentionally; I simply was speaking directly from "Source" and not even aware of what I was saying. Words and ideas just flowed and felt aligned. I was walking this life from a different perspective.

Everything is energy and the reality of this statement was hitting home like never before. I was seeing life from an energetic vantage point. I was feeling life from a frequency vibration. I was interacting with life from an observer's perspective. I felt my very cells' energy increasing. Sometimes this took my breath away.

Often, I felt surreal, such as when in the practice of observing I also observe myself from different perspectives. One evening, as I was feeling this disconnectedness, I closed my eyes and intentionally played the observer.

- What would happen if I observed me from outside my house?
- What would happen if I observed me from outside my city?
- What would happen if I observed me from outside my county?
- What would happen if I observed me from outside my state?
- What would happen if I observed me from outside my country?
- What would happen if I observed me from outside my world?
- What would happen if I observed me from outside my universe?
- And so on...

I found myself floating just outside a realm of pure energy and floating right in front of me was a beautiful white dragon. She had a long, elegant tail and was a blend of pure white, snow white, pearl white, frosty white, and all with a translucent glow. Her wings were transparent with hints of pink, blue, yellow, and white running through and she had long horns shooting straight up with a small energy shape between them that looked like an infinity sign. She stood there, holding the universe between her hands.

“Hello and welcome to your source of true power.”

Her voice was like a purr as she spoke so lovingly.

“I am the Source Dragon here to guide you so you will not get lost on this profound Soul Quest. I will hold you as your sense of self dissolves. During this time, you will experience a state of pure unity, where you realize you are indistinguishable from all existence, a kind of cosmic consciousness or infinite awareness.

Here, you will experience a form of "knowing" that transcends thought or sensory input. You will exist in a state where beginnings, ends, locations, or durations have no meaning. This is the eternal "now," where all events, possibilities, and states coexist without distinction.”

I was so in awe of this magnificent creature while my heart felt like it was pulling me home. Pulling me forward into the web of energy pulsing in front of me. I felt the dragon lift me on her back and together we went into the nexus of this web.

I became one with an infinite field of potential and the very concept of "experience" was irrelevant. I was dissolving into this source, an ecstatic, infinite oneness that defies description but feels like the ultimate truth. I was home.

As I tried to take this all in, I also knew my humanness would not be able to describe this feeling of awe, peace, and terror as the boundaries of myself and my known reality vanished. It was like infinite love and nothingness, both existing simultaneously. I was in a state of pure existence or awareness without form or limit.

I began to notice that the white Source Dragon was gently flying me out of the matrix of Source. My heart was breaking as I longed to return to where I knew I belonged.

I realized she was taking me back. “This experience has ignited your Mitochondria even more, the energy within each cell of your body responsible for maximum health. This was necessary in order for you to withstand the experience you just had. Without this you might not have had a way to ‘return.’ “

This was shocking information. I took a deep breath and opened my eyes to discover I was on my living room couch and had been in this state of "being" for six hours. I immediately grabbed my journal to document what just happened as best I could. It felt as though I had woken from a dream I could not fully articulate, but the feeling lingered in my heart.

What I realized was that I now had a certainty about me. A feeling of knowing without having to explain, justify, or understand. It simply is and I also now know that where we all come from is beyond the understanding of humans experiencing life on earth. We live in contrast that has the energy of fear, anger, sadness, shame, guilt and more. These emotions and this contrast simply do not exist past this third dimensional energetic state. It is those very feelings, those vibrations, that we chose to experience. We are energy in motion (e-motion) and feeling what we feel is a magnificent gift to us and to the Universe. We are the creators born from source consciousness with the ability to connect to something greater than us when we are willing to let go of the belief that this is the only reality there is.

When I allowed myself to dream again and believe in the dragons and their gifts, I allowed the magic of the Universe to be presented to me in such beautiful ways. The dragons are all around me and they are all around you waiting to be invited in to support you with nothing but pure unconditional love.

I invite you to believe in magic. I invite you to explore the elementals. I invite you to imagine yourself as part of the quantum dimensions of existence. I invite you to let these in with love and watch how your world can change.

Dragon Meditations

A collective meditation – changing the world - inspired by the dragons created by Diana Cooper and her Dragon oracle cards.

Sit back comfortably, arms uncrossed, feet flat on the ground.

Gently close your eyes and breathe deeply, knowing that you are now connecting with the consciousness of the elements of earth.

Continue breathing deeply at your own rhythm.

I wonder what you might experience today, in your meditation as you feel yourself traveling above the earth and moving around the world. As you pass over continent by continent can you see the entire world living in peace, harmony and oneness? Notice how this image and feeling becomes ever more crystal clear in your vision and crystal pure in your heart.

As you move through your quest, feel free to ask for assistance.

Ask the blue air dragons to blow this vision into the minds of those in power world-wide. Ask them to touch the hearts of business leaders filling them with good will and heart-centered actions. Ask them to touch the teaching institutions with divine wisdom and pure intentions.

Ask the earth dragons to heal the land, diving deep into the earth where there has been conflict and shootings to purify and transmute the negative energy stuck there. Ask them to pour their healing essence into the Ley Lines where they have been damaged or broken, healing the fabric of mother earth. Marvel at their current mission to create new lines at the various dimensions of human ascension.

How might it feel to ask the angels to touch the heart of everyone in the world and to sing a song of peace over us all?

Ask the unicorns to shower the entire world with pure white light to raise the frequency everywhere.

Ask the earth-guides, earth-angels, and earth-teachers to release all that weighs them down and to step into their light freely and clearly.

Know that this is good. Know that this is true. And in the asking, know that this is so.

Meditation – 00 Where Has All the Magic Gone?

Find yourself a comfortable position, sitting or lying down. Uncross your arms and legs and, if possible, place your feet flat on the ground.

Gently close your eyes and breathe deeply, knowing that you are now connecting with the consciousness of the elements of earth. Breath in life force energy, breath out compassion. Breath in the gift of life, breath out the gift for nature.

Continue breathing deeply at your own rhythm.

Imagine yourself in a most peaceful place in nature.

Find the perfect spot to lay down in as you take in the beauty of mother nature

Notice the colors around you.

- Maybe there are trees – notice the trunk, the branches, the leaves. Do you hear the breeze passing through the branches?
- Is there grass? How tall, how lush? What is the color? How does the light reflect off each blade? Can you smell the very dirt around you?

- Look at the sky. What is the color? Are there clouds? What do they look like? Can you feel the sun's warmth on your face?
- What are the sounds around you? Is there a breeze? Are there birds? Maybe the sound of a stream?

Imagine you have the power to change the colors. Maybe see different hues. There could be shades you've never seen before.

Look around you now and with your hands, imagine you are pulling back a veil that is over your scenery and in doing so, the colors become more vivid. The depth of everything appears more profound.

- Maybe the trees seem to be breathing and the branches sway like a conductor while the leaves dance to a music you had not heard before.

- The grass seems to pulse, as though the earth itself is breathing and the landscape ebbs and flows with each breath in and out.

- The sky seems to transform into a land not seen before. Fairies, angels, and dragons are flowing around, dancing and laughing and thrilled that you see them.

Look around and notice how this perfect place has a melody and it is singing to you. Close your eyes in this moment. I wonder how differently you feel right now.

This is the magic you can create and in knowing this to be true, you also know this has always been here waiting for you.

Recording **-** https://youtu.be/VksWzvzRUtM

Meditation – 01 Elementals and Dimensions

Sit back comfortably, arms uncrossed, feet flat on the ground.

Gently close your eyes and breathe deeply, knowing that you are now connecting with the consciousness of the elements of earth.

Continue breathing deeply at your own rhythm.

As you breathe, imagine you are standing on a mountain top where you can see the earth from any direction and she is glorious.

Turn to face the East. Feel the air fresh and clear as this is where the element of new beginnings, birth, and renewal is born.

Say softly, in your mind or out loud, "Hello, East! Spirit of the morning, grant me clarity and inspiration in my daily life."

Feel the breeze pick up around you, gently touching you like the breath of fairies. Feel their free-spirited essence with moments of elusiveness. Just like a breath of fresh air, this elemental clears the space for you with lightness and movement, it is a gateway to the Universe, and your life force energy.

Turn now to the south. Feel the essence of growth, warmth, summer, and the element of Fire.

Find yourself feeling comfort in this inviting heat and whisper to yourself, "Hello, South! Protector of the home, protect me from harm and guide me in my endeavors."

Realize that the fire from the south is here to warm your heart, protect your sphere, and accelerate your transformation. Everything fire touches crystallizes and changes what once was into something spectacular. Feel the comfort from fire, sitting around the campfire and sharing stories, roasting marshmallows, and poking the embers to keep warmth going.

Know that, because you are feeling the safety and warmth from the South, you are confident in turning now to face the West. Here is where you go to feel introspection. Imagine what it is like to release as this is where the end of a cycle, maturity, and the element of Water supports your growth. As you hear the sound of the gentle waves lapping at the shore, say to yourself, "Hello, West! Guardian of the evening, bless my journey and protect me as I travel."

Remember now that with Water you feel yourself swimming in its flow as it holds the movement of your emotions, and you experience emotive healing, balance, intuition, creativity, and inner peace. With the current of the water element there is no resistance, only a gently flow toward your destiny.

I wonder what it would be like now to slowly turn toward the North where you find wisdom, stability, winter, and the element of Earth.

Gaia holds the deepest and oldest wisdom while re-birthing anew every day. She holds the consciousness of symbiotic living for you, her creatures, and herself. Whisper now, “Hello, North! Guardian of the Earth, bring forth for me the strength and wisdom of the land."

The Earth elemental is ancient, deep, and unshakable. Feel yourself as you realize you are anchored to the earth, smell the dirt, and the aroma of fresh leaves. Know that you are one with earth elementals. Mother Earth brings rationality and the basis of stability. Invoke this elemental and feel it bring in diligence. Give yourself permission to get curious and look for the lesson and the wisdom.

Take a deep breath in as it is now time for you to move on, bringing the elements with you, integrated into your soul.

Slowly open your eyes, stretch a bit, come back from this experience.

Recording: https://youtu.be/Ja30aZHEddI

Meditation – 03 Earth Dragon

Sit like an ancient redwood: spine straight, roots plunging deep into the heart of the planet. Uncross everything. Let your arms rest heavy and open, palms turned down into the soil of your own body.

Close your eyes.

Breathe in the wild, green fire of life itself... slow, deliberate, unstoppable. Breathe out a river of gratitude that pours straight into the core of Gaia. Inhale the pulse of the Earth. Exhale your heartbeat back into Her. Feel the rhythm lock: yours and Hers, one drum.

With every breath, sink. Not falling; merging. Your bones become stone. Your blood becomes river. Your breath becomes wind through ten billion leaves.

Now you stand barefoot in a cathedral of old-growth forest. The air is so thick with aliveness it hums against your skin. Moss drinks starlight. Every root beneath you sing in a language older than words.

From the sky of emerald shadows, she arrives.

A magnificent Earth Dragon, scales the color of fertile soil after rain, veined with rivers of liquid sapphire light. Her wings are ancient forests; her eyes are deep glacial lakes that have never forgotten the stars.

She lands without a sound, yet the ground thrums with welcome. Bow, not in submission, but in recognition of equals.

Speak your true name, the one that existed before your first cry on this planet. She answers with a voice like tectonic plates caressing one another:

“I am the Weaver of Ley. I sang the first grid of light into the molten body of this world. These liquid blue arteries you feel beneath your feet are my veins and yours. When they are wounded, you bleed. When you are healed, I sing.”

Feel Her compassion: vast, fierce, inexhaustible. She shows you how She moves mountains of stagnant grief, human and planetary, sweeping them aside like autumn leaves so that seedlings of light can break through.

Walk with Her now. Every step is a prayer. Wherever old pain, pollution, or forgotten war energy lies knotted in the land, she exhales slow emerald fire.

Watch: debris dissolves, darkness transmutes, coal of suffering flashes into liquid diamond-blue life force that instantly streams back into the Ley Lines, making them glow brighter, stronger, wilder.

Feel it in your own body. Every psychic splinter, every inherited wound, every place you carried the world's sorrow without knowing it, she gently, relentlessly burns it clean. You become lighter than you have ever been, yet more solid, like a mountain that learned how to dance.

She pauses at a great crossroads of Ley Lines, a planetary chakra pulsing weakly under centuries of harm. Look into Her eyes. Ask, with all the authority of your awakened soul:

"Great Guardian, unblock and restore the living veins of Gaia.

Let the blue fire run free again."

She bows Her massive head until Her forehead touches yours. A single tear of liquid starlight falls from Her eye into your heart. In that moment, every Ley Line on Earth flares back to full brilliance.

You feel the surge race through your spine, your legs, the soles of your feet, a planetary orgasm of healing.

The forest roars in celebration. Every tree, every stone, every ancestor standing behind your cheers.

Turn to Her. Place your hands on the warm earth of Her brow and kiss the place where the third eye of the planet beats. Speak from the throne of your own sovereign heart:

“Thank you, Earth Dragon, Sister of Root and Star. I remember now: to love the Earth is to love myself, and to love myself is to heal the Earth. I accept my place on your council of guardians.”

She spreads wings of living cedar and light, rises in a spiral of emerald and gold, and with the promise:

“I am always here. Walk gently, burn brightly, and the grid will answer your footfalls.”

Feel Her become the wind, become the roots, become the river inside your veins.

Take one last breath that draws the entire planet into your chest...and release it as a vow. Open your eyes.

The healing you just received is not a gift you were given. It is the power you have remembered you always carried.

Stand up. Walk outside today and touch a tree, a stone, running water, bare earth. Whisper, “I’m back.”

The Earth Dragon hears you. The Ley Lines light up beneath your feet. And the age of true co-creation has begun.

Recording - https://youtu.be/0gzJFizp0-Q

Meditation – 04 Fire and Water Dragon

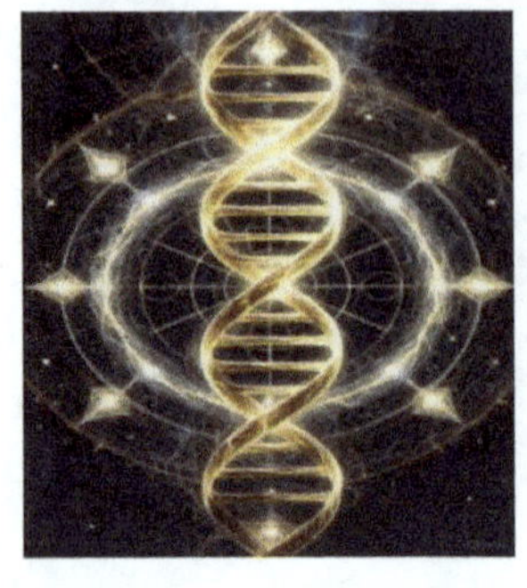

Sit or lie down in a place that feels sacred to you. Spine straight, as though a column of star-fire runs through you. Place one hand on your heart, one hand on your lower belly: the ancient gateways of creation. Close your eyes.

Breathe in for 5... hold for 5... exhale for 8. Again. And again. Each exhale is an offering; each inhale is the universe accepting it.

Imagine now, around your body, an ocean of living color begins to rise.

Notice how at first comes Blue: deep midnight-cobalt, the color of the womb of galaxies. It pours over you like liquid peace. Feel every cell sigh open. Inside your DNA, forgotten strands begin to hum, uncoiling like sleeping serpents tasting freedom for the first time in millennia.

The blue deepens, then suddenly ignites into radiant Yellow: solar fire, pure divine intelligence. Your temperature rises, but it is not heat; it is remembrance. You are light remembering it chose to become a body.

Yellow softens into living Orange: the color of the sacred second chakra, molten creativity. Old blockages in your lineage, your womb or seed, your right to feel and to create, melt like ancient ice in a sudden spring. A quiet, unstoppable Zen fire spreads through your pelvis and belly: the joy of becoming.

Now Red floods in, thick as dragon's blood. It is not aggression; it is pure life-force, the original passion that said, "Let there be." Feel it surge through every vein, kissing each cell awake. Your heartbeat becomes a drum announcing the return of a sovereign creator.

Just when the heat feels almost too much, White descends blinding, alchemical, supernova white. It is the fusion point. Past and future collapse into one eternal NOW inside your DNA. Every base pair flashes, rewrites, upgrades. You are literally becoming a new frequency while still wearing this beloved body.

A soft rain of diamond-clear water now falls, cooling, washing, baptizing. Through the curtain of rain, you see a perfect rainbow bridge. From its center steps the Fire-and-Water Dragon.

One half of his colossal body blazes with the entire spectrum of flame: crimson, magma-orange, sun-gold. The other half flows with living ocean: sapphire, aqua, moon-silver. Where the two halves meet along his spine, steam rises in the shape of ascending double helices: your new DNA being born in real time.

He lowers his massive head until his third eye touches yours. A single tear of liquid starlight falls from his eye into your crown and streams down every strand of your genetic code.

He speaks, and every atom in your body hears:

"Child of the First Breath, I am the union of all opposites that ever pretended to be separate. Today I rewrite the story written in your blood. No more inherited limitation. No more ancestral fear disguised as fate. Only the original blueprint: limitless, luminous, free."

Feel his wings, one of fire, one of water, enfold you completely. Inside that embrace, laughter erupts from your depths: pure, childlike, unstoppable. You are suddenly, shockingly alive, as if you have never truly breathed until this moment.

Old timelines, old wounds, old identities flake off like burnt paper and dissolve in the rain. Beneath them shines the new you: crystalline, radiant, playful, powerful beyond measure.

The Dragon breathes once more: a single breath that is both inferno and tsunami. It enters through your crown, spirals down your spine, and explodes outward as a nova of rainbow fire from every pore.

You are recoded. You are reborn. You are magnificent, and you know it in your bones.

Stay in his embrace as long as you wish, laughing, crying, roaring with joy.

When the moment feels complete, place your hands over your heart and speak directly to him:

“Thank you, Beloved Fire-and-Water, for burning away what was never true and flooding me with what has always been. I accept my original codes. I step forward as the creator I was born to be.”

He bows; wings sweeping galaxies and becomes pure light that settles as a living helix inside your heart center.

Take three slow breaths, feeling your new frequency anchor into every cell. Wiggle fingers and toes. Smile the smile of someone who just remembered they are divine.

Open your eyes.

Look around. The world is suddenly brighter, more alive, because you are.

Carry this fire. Carry this water. Walk as the living rainbow bridge from now on.

You are the new human. And you have only just begun.

Recording – https://youtu.be/58fCJRExiYY

Meditation – 05 Fire Dragon

Find a quiet place where you won't be disturbed. Allow yourself to settle in, whether sitting or lying down. Close your eyes gently.

Bring your attention to your breath. Feel the rhythm of life moving through you, steady and constant. With each inhale, invite calm. With each exhale, release tension. Let your body soften and relax completely.

Imagine yourself gazing into a vast sky at sunset. The sun dips toward the horizon, painting the clouds in brilliant shades of crimson and gold. The entire landscape glows under this fiery red light, a world transformed by the power of dusk.

As you watch, notice one cloud moving closer. Slowly, it begins to take shape. Its edges sharpen, its color deepens, until you see it clearly, a magnificent Fire Dragon, shimmering in hues of scarlet and gold.

He descends gracefully, landing before you with a presence that feels both fierce and tender. Majestic and powerful, yet his eyes hold infinite wisdom. He bows in greeting, and you feel honored by his gesture.

The dragon invites you to sit beside him. As you move closer, imagine sensing the warmth radiating from his body, a heat that feels cleansing rather than burning. His breath flows like a lullaby, soft, steady, and strong.

He speaks to you in a voice that resonates deep within your soul: “I am the element of purification and release. I am here to guide you to what has been hidden, so you may let it go.”

You now realize that you are leaning gently against his warm body. Feel the rise and fall of his breath and notice how your own breathing begins to match his rhythm. You are safe. You are held.

Before you, the dragon exhales a stream of flame onto the earth, creating a glowing patch of firelight. Within this fiery circle, a story begins to unfold, a memory from long ago. Perhaps it is something you have carried unknowingly, a shadow lingering in your lineage, or an old wound buried deep in your soul.

Watch as this energy reveals itself. Notice its texture, its weight. Feel its presence without judgment. And now, see the dragon’s flames consume it, burning away the heaviness, dissolving the patterns that no longer serve you.

As the fire purifies, sense your body letting go. The old energy melts into nothingness, and in its place, a new light begins to emerge, a vision of freedom, of possibility, of who you truly are.

Celebrate this transformation. Feel the shift from heaviness to lightness, from burden to liberation. This is your essence, unbound, radiant, whole.

Watch as the flames fade now, leaving only a gentle warmth in your heart. You turn to thank the Fire Dragon, but he is gone. Yet his gift remains, a deep, glowing warmth within your soul, yours to keep forever.

Take a deep breath in. Slowly exhale. Stretch your arms toward the sky. When you are ready, open your eyes.

Welcome back. You are whole. You are free.

Recording **–** https://youtu.be/FoBf7WZHmd0

Meditation – 07 Black Dragon of Saturn

Let's begin by finding a quiet space where you will not be disturbed. Allow yourself to settle in, whether sitting or lying down, choose what feels most comfortable.

Gently close your eyes.

Bring your awareness to your breath. Feel the rhythm of life moving through you, steady and eternal. Inhale deeply… exhale slowly… and let each breath draw you deeper into relaxation.

Sink into the chair, couch, or floor beneath you. Feel the weight of your body supported completely.

As you breathe, notice the cadence of your life force—the ebb and flow, the rise and fall. In your mind's eye, imagine each breath forming soft puffs of cloud, merging with the moisture in the darkness around you. These clouds gather, creating a cushion of vapor, lifting you gently upward.

Feel yourself enveloped in these misty blankets of your own creation. Notice the contrast, the luminous fog against the infinite blackness of night. The darkness moves, alive with currents. Soon you realize these currents are stirred by the wings of a majestic being, a Black Dragon, shimmering like obsidian, powerful and graceful.

She lands upon your cloud with silent strength. Her eyes: ancient, wise, and full of mystery meet yours. You create space for her presence and greet her with reverence. She speaks:

“I am the Black Dragon of Saturn. I am the keeper of balance between chaos and transformation. I guide those who seek to embrace their shadow and emerge reborn. Come with me, and together we will journey to Saturn, a sanctuary where your hidden self can be revealed and transmuted into strength, wisdom, and spiritual light.”

Imagine feeling her invitation resonate within you. With trust, you climb onto her back, nestling securely against her scales.

The dragon launches into the cosmos, swift and powerful. Hear the rush of wind, feel the exhilaration as Earth falls away and the vastness of space surrounds you. Stars blur past as Saturn’s rings come into view, glowing like celestial ribbons.

She lands upon a moon nestled within Saturn’s rings. The landscape shimmers with hues of silver and gold. Listen to the whispering storms that dance along the rings. Ahead, a structure rises, a temple of light, and before it stands a luminous being Seraphina, an angel of the Seraphim.

Seraphina beckons you inside. You enter and sit upon a soft cushion, surrendering to her presence. Her voice is like music:

"Through my eyes, behold the infinite glory of the Divine, so vast, so radiant, it cannot be contained by any realm. You are a spark of this magnificence. Today, you are attuned to its frequency."

Feel her blessing permeate your being, your heart, your mind, your very DNA. Waves of light ripple through you, dissolving old patterns, awakening new strength. You realize you are being reborn.

Breathe deeply. Let this truth settle into every cell: You are miraculous.

Notice the Black Dragon nudging you gently, it is time to return. You thank Seraphina with gratitude beyond words and mount the dragon once more. The flight home is serene, carrying you through starlit silence.

As you arrive, dismount and embrace the Black Dragon. Feel her power, her grace, her eternal presence. Watch as she ascends into the clouds, leaving you with the gift of transformation.

Take a moment to wonder: What would it be like to carry this experience into your everyday life?

Now, slowly bring your awareness back. Wiggle your toes, your fingers. Take a deep breath and gently open your eyes.

Welcome back—renewed, reborn, and radiant.

Recording – https://youtu.be/_MSpAuS_JdA

Meditation – 08 Green Dragon

Find yourself a comfortable and quiet spot. Relax and feel the tension in every muscle release from the top of your head, and ripple down through the tips of your toes. If you are seated, place both feet on the ground. Place your hands face down on your thighs, allowing you to remain grounded. Gently close your eyes or softly stare ahead.

Imagine, slightly above your head a soft white cloud moving closer and closer. As it descends feel the coolness of this cloud seeping through the top of your head, releasing any remaining tension. Feel what it might be like for it to slowly move down the back of your head, the front of your head. Feel the sensation as your jaw relaxes, your neck releases tension and your vocal cords are untensed. The cloud continues down your body, your arms, your stomach relaxing and cooling any tension on its way. Moving down your thighs, calves, ankles, and feet. Loosening tension along the way and finally out, connecting with mother earth.

I wonder what would it be like when you notice that there are sounds and smells of nature entering your sphere? Maybe the smell of trees, the odor of the sea, the smell of moss, or wildflowers all around you.

Notice that you are becoming aware of the birds, insects, or the rustling of animals curious about you.

Realize that you are seeing this scenery more and more clearly as it becomes more and more in focus for you and as you look around, see nestled on a rock a green dragon watching you enter her realm.

Walk up to her and take note of the tones of her color, the tattoos on her legs, the cadence of her breathing. She gracefully steps off the rock and allows you to pet her, feeling her skin and her wings. She lets out a quiet purr.

“I am the Green Dragon here to introduce you to the consciousness of Gaia and the world she creates. Walk with me as we listen to her together.”

As you begin to walk you can hear the wisdom of the earth rise up through your body and into your mind. You can feel the wonders of this world within you and, as you listen to secrets spoken only to you, you know you are unlocking sacred secrets, and you are connecting with nature.

As you listen you begin to truly understand you are one with all that is around you. It feeds you and you feed it.

The Green Dragon leads you beside a brook and invites you to sit in the soft grass. She touches your heart and whispers, “you are connected to all you see and all you can imagine. The wisdom you seek and the answers to your questions lie here, locked in your heart for safe keeping. You simply need to touch this with love and trust, and all will unfold before you. Gaia is here to keep the balance of nature in check, and you are part of that great work.”

Imagine how it feels as the consciousness of Gaia becomes the consciousness of you. You and she are one and she now brings all her knowing into you.

Find yourself sitting quietly for a moment with these words and with these feelings as you watch the Green Dragon melt into the scenery, leaving behind a smile of knowing and of love.

Take a deep breath in and slowly open your eyes. Take a stretch, wiggle your fingers, stretch your toes, and twitch your nose.

You are ancient wisdom.

Welcome back.

Recording **-** https://youtu.be/EZj1Ujhbl8Q

Meditation – 09 Golden Christed Dragon

Find a quiet, comfortable place where you will not be disturbed. Sit with both feet flat on the ground, spine straight but relaxed, hands resting palm-down on your thighs (grounded, receptive, open).

Close your eyes gently or let your gaze soften.

Breathe in slowly for 4... hold for 4... exhale for 7.

Repeat three more times, letting each breath out carry away the day's energy.

I wonder if you can simply watch the breath. Thoughts come, let them drift past like clouds in a vast sky. You do not need to follow them.

As you breathe, notice the crown of your head soften and open, as though a thousand-petaled lotus blooms at the top of your skull. From infinite space above, a warm, living golden-white light begins to pour in gentle, yet unstoppable. It enters through the crown and immediately dissolves every knot of tension across the scalp. It flows down the back of the head, the forehead, the temples; the eyes grow heavy and peaceful, the jaw unhinges and hangs loose, the throat opens like a chalice.

Feel yourself relax even more as the light continues downward. Shoulders drop, arms grow weightless, chest expands, belly softens, spine lengthens. It moves through hips, thighs, knees, calves, ankles, and finally streams out the soles of your feet, rooting you deep into the living heart of Mother Earth while simultaneously connecting you to the Father-Mother Source above.

You are now a clear column of golden light.

Within this column, the light begins to condense and take form.

As you watch this transform you realize that before you, radiant and immense yet tender, a magnificent Golden Dragon appears. Her scales are liquid sunlight; her eyes hold the gentle authority of eternity. She inclines her great head in a gesture of reverence and speaks, not with words that the mind translates, but directly into your heart:

"I am the Christed Dragon of the Golden Ray. I bring you the living presence of the Christ energy."

From the center of her chest, a sphere of rose-gold fire pulses once, twice, and then expands into an ocean of liquid light that pours over and into you. It is warm, but not merely warm: it is the temperature of being completely seen and completely loved at the same moment.

As this Christed light touches your skin, something extraordinary happens.

Suddenly, crystalline clarity descends. Every inner voice, every looping thought, every subtle murmur of self-doubt or ancient shame...stops.

Not suppressed. Not pushed away. They simply dissolve, the way shadows vanish the instant the sun rises.

What remains is silence so vast and luminous that it feels like the first moment the universe ever breathed.

Only peace. Only presence. Only the eternal Now.

And in that clarity, a second wave arises, this one softer, deeper, more intimate. A sense of being deeply, unspeakably known.

Every secret you ever buried, every moment you felt unworthy, every wound you pretended did not hurt, everything is laid bare, yet not to judgment.

The gaze that meets you is the gaze of the One who was with you in the womb, who walked beside you through every dark valley, who knelt in Gethsemane and whispered, “Even this I carry with you.”

And in the same instant that you are fully seen, you are fully forgiven, not as an act of condescension, but as the simple recognition that there was never anything to forgive.

The Christed Dragon's heart-fire pours the balm of absolute mercy into your every cell.

You feel the precise moment the ancient weight lifts from your shoulders, your chest, your DNA itself.

Tears may come—not from sorrow, but from the unbearable sweetness of coming home to a home you never truly left.

The Golden Dragon lowers her great head until her forehead touches yours. A silent transmission passes between you: the living remembrance that you are the Beloved.

Golden Christ Light Codes—spirals and geometries of pure resurrection frequency stream from her third eye into yours, then cascade down through every chakra, every meridian, every strand of DNA.

They are rewriting you at the quantum level, awakening the original template: the Child of God you were before the world taught you otherwise.

You hear, or rather feel, the whisper of countless dragons and angelic hosts singing in one voice:

"You are loved without condition.

You are held in the Heart of the Christ energy forever.

Never again will you walk in darkness, for the Light has recognized itself as You."

Remain in this embrace as long as you wish. Time has ceased to matter.

When you feel complete, watch as the Golden Christed Dragon smiles, a smile that is both fierce and infinitely tender, and slowly dissolves back into the living golden light that now fills and surrounds you. Yet she does not leave. She has become the very atmosphere of your being.

Take one slow, deep breath, feeling this new frequency settle into your bones.

Wiggle your fingers and toes.

Gently stretch.

Open your eyes when you are ready.

Wherever you go now, the Christed Dragon walks within you.

The crystalline clarity and the knowing-forgiveness remain, quiet flames that no outer circumstance can extinguish.

Welcome home, Beloved.

You are forever changed.

And you were always, already, whole.

Recording – https://youtu.be/lGSzPgploGI

Meditation – 10 Orange Dragon

Find yourself a comfortable, quiet spot where you will not be disturbed. Sit with both feet flat on the ground, spine tall but relaxed. Place your hands palms down on your thighs, anchoring you to the earth. Gently close your eyes or soften your gaze.

Take a slow, delicious breath in for 4 counts... hold for 4... and release for 7.

Repeat three more times, letting each exhale carry away anything that feels heavy or separate from love. With every breath, thoughts may drift by like clouds. Let them pass. You are simply here, breathing, arriving.

Imagine witnessing yourself in a sacred circle of soft golden-orange light. You are not alone. All around you, in a wide, gentle ring, sit beings of every color, every age, every walk of life. Some you know, many you have never met, yet all are here with you now, breathing in the same rhythm. I invite you to feel the quiet power of this circle. Feel the invisible threads of light that already connect every heart.

In the center of the circle burns a single candle, its flame alive with dancing orange fire. Watch the flame. Let your breath and its flicker fall into the same easy cadence. In...the flame rises. Out...the flame settles. In...out...together.

As you breathe with the flame you realize an Orange Dragon steps gracefully out of the fire. Its scales shimmer like molten sunset, its eyes deep pools of welcoming warmth. It does not stand above you; it settles into the circle as your equal, wings folded softly, tail curled in gentle companionship.

The dragon's gaze meets yours, and in that moment you feel your navel chakra awaken: a warm, spinning sun just below your belly button. This is the sacred fire of relatedness, of creativity, of "we."

The dragon speaks, its voice like honeyed embers:

"Beloved, I do not come to you from outside. I rise from within you, for I am the part of you that remembers we were never separate. Look around this circle. See the divine wearing a thousand faces.

See the same longing for belonging in every set of eyes. See how every story, every skin tone, every language is a unique note in one great song the universe is singing through us.

I live in your navel fire so that I may work through you. When you walk among others, I walk with you. When you listen, I help you hear the heartbeat beneath the words. When walls of fear or judgment rise, I breathe my gentle orange flame and they melt into doorways.

Feel me now, spinning warmly in your center. With every breath, I send tendrils of light from your navel to every being in this circle...and beyond it...to every soul you will ever meet.

We are the bridge-builders. We are the wall-dissolvers. We are the ones who look across any divide and say, 'There goes my brother, my sister, my own heart in another form.'"

As the dragon speaks, the circle of light around you brightens. You see golden-orange threads weaving from your navel to every other navel in the circle, then outward like ripples: across streets, oceans, borders, centuries. The threads hum with joy. Laughter rises. Hands reach out. Strangers become family. Differences become the very brushstrokes of a masterpiece.

The dragon leans closer, eyes sparkling.

"Carry this fire when you leave this circle. Let it glow behind every smile you give. Let it soften every judgment before it forms. Let it remind you, again and again:

There is no ‘other.’ There is only us, rejoicing in our infinite expressions. Together, we are the new world remembering itself.”

Feel the truth of this settle into your bones. Feel the warmth pool in your navel and radiate outward until your whole body is glowing like a lantern of belonging.

The Orange Dragon smiles, bows its great head in gratitude, and gently dissolves back into the candle flame, leaving its living ember inside you.

The circle of beings around you begins to fade, but the threads remain: bright, unbreakable, pulsing with love.

Take one more deep breath in...and as you exhale, imagine blowing out the candle with a soft, deliberate breath.

Wiggle your fingers and toes. Stretch your arms overhead. Roll your shoulders. Smile.

Open your eyes.

Welcome back, bridge-builder. The Orange Dragon is still spinning warmly in your navel, working through you, now and always.

Whenever you need to remember the great “We,” simply place a hand on your belly, breathe, and feel the circle re-form. You are never alone. You are the connection the world has been waiting for.

Recording – https://youtu.be/PqOunlAb4rU

Meditation – 11 Magenta Dragon

Find yourself a comfortable and quiet spot. Relax and feel the tension in every muscle release from the top of your head, and ripple down through the tips of your toes. If you are seated, place both feet on the ground. Place your hands face down on your thighs, allowing you to remain grounded.

Gently close your eyes or softly stare ahead.

Take in a full breath, breathe deeply into your belly.

Hold that to the count of 4.

And exhale to the count of 7, pushing the air out from the bottom of your belly.

Breathe in again to the count of 4.

Hold that to the count of 4.

And breathe out to the count of 7.

Remember to focus on your breathing.

This breath is not air; it is the original dragon fire of your soul returning home.

With every exhale, feel molten gold pour from the crown of your head down through every cell, melting tension, melting fear, melting centuries of forgetting.

You are not relaxing. You are igniting.

I wonder what it would be like in your inner vision, you saw a vast cathedral of night open before you.

Imagine walls of living amethyst rising into infinity. Silken banners of deep magenta and star-fire ripple like dragon wings in a cosmic wind. Suppose before you is a throne, not of gold, but of living light, carved for a sovereign being who is only now remembering their name.

Imagine yourself stepping forward. Sit. Claim it.

Across from you rises an altar forged from a single slab of star-born obsidian. Notice upon it burns an eternal violet flame. Crystals of every color hum in perfect geometry.

Find yourself looking at a great magenta dragon, scales shimmering with galaxies, landing without sound. Her eyes are twin supernovae. When she speaks, the entire universe leans in to listen.

"Beloved Ancient One, you did not lose your memory. You hid your brilliance inside this human form so that you could experience the indescribable glory of finding yourself again, and in that finding, set the worlds on fire.

I am the Magenta Dragon, Keeper of the First Flame. I have come because you called, because the moment of your full remembrance has arrived.

Today we burn away the illusion of separation. Today you reclaim the throne that was never taken, only forgotten.

I invite you to lift your hands. Feel the heat rising in your palms, ancient, familiar, unstoppable."

The dragon breathes a single breath of living magenta fire across your chest. Watch now:

Every story of unworthiness, every scar of shame, every chain of guilt, every mask you wore to survive, they rise from your cells like dark smoke, drawn irresistibly into the violet flame.

Do not flinch. This is not pain leaving. This is power returning.

Imagine how it feels as you witness the smoke condense into a perfect sphere of night between your hands. All that was never truly you, now held in mercy, ready for transmutation.

The dragon's voice thunders softly inside your bones:

"Behold, I make all things new."

She exhales again, pure white gold dragon fire. The sphere ignites. In a single heartbeat it transmutes into a radiant star of crystalline diamond light, blazing with every color that has ever existed and some that have never been named.

She places this newborn star directly into your heart.

Feel it. It is not a stone. It is the original seed of your soul, returned, upgraded, awake.

A tidal wave of remembering floods you:

You are not a human seeking enlightenment. You are an ancient dragon of divine origin wearing a human cloak for one magnificent incarnation. You came to burn away the dream of separation and to love this world so fiercely that it remembers it is God.

The dragon bows, wings spreading across all dimensions.

Find yourself rising from the throne. No longer seeker. Sovereign. Radiant. Unforgotten.

Take one final breath that fills every star in the cosmos.

Exhale as the roar of a thousand dragons.

Open your eyes.

The world looks different now, because you are different. Everything you touch today will remember it is sacred. Every heartbeat is a drumbeat announcing your return.

Stand up. Stretch your magnificent wings (even if the world still calls them arms). Smile like the unstoppable force you have always been.

Welcome home, Dragon.

The age of forgetting is over.

The age of blazing has begun.

Recording – https://youtu.be/SXPnhtPR80I

Meditation – 12 Sunshine Yellow Dragon

Find a quiet, comfortable place where you will not be disturbed. Sit or lie down, whichever feels best. If you are seated, let both feet rest flat on the floor. Place your hands palms down on your thighs or simply let them rest wherever they feel grounded and at peace.

Close your eyes gently or soften your gaze. Take a slow, deep breath in...filling your belly first, then your chest. Hold for a gentle count of 4. And now exhale slowly for a count of 7, letting every last bit of air leave as though you are releasing anything that no longer serves you.

Again...breathe in...hold...and exhale fully. One more time...in... hold...and release.

I invite you now to allow your breath to find its own natural rhythm. With each exhale, feel your body grow heavier, more relaxed, more supported by the earth beneath you.

I wonder...what would it be like when you realize there is a tender, warm, sunshine-yellow glow appearing just above your head. It is soft like morning light, yet alive with gentle power.

Imagine feeling this golden-yellow radiance begin to pour slowly downward, like warm honey, seeping into the crown of your head, melting away any tension, any worry, any old thought ready to dissolve.

Feel this light travel down through your mind, soothing every thought

Down your neck...relaxing the vagus nerve that carries peace throughout your entire system.

Down your shoulders, arms, and hands.

Down your spine...filling your chest and heart with radiant warmth...flowing into your belly, hips, legs, and all the way to the tips of your toes.

Notice how your whole being is bathed in sunshine yellow light, safe, held, and deeply loved.

Realize as you rest in this glow, you are becoming aware of its source. High above you circle the most gentle and compassionate of all dragons: a magnificent Sunshine Yellow Dragon. Its scales shimmer like liquid sunlight, its eyes are pools of infinite kindness, and its vast wings spread wide in blessing.

Imagine this beautiful being pouring its light into you, cleansing, uplifting, and awakening within you a profound remembrance:

Every creature upon this Earth is sacred.

Imagine the dragon's energy now carrying gentle codes of light directly into your heart and into every cell of your body. These are upgrades of compassion, upgrades of understanding. Your DNA softly rewinds and re-encodes with the remembering that all life is connected, that every paw, hoof, wing, and fin is part of the same great song.

With this upgrade comes a new responsibility and a new gift:

You have become a living bridge of light. Sunshine Yellow Dragons may now travel along the pathway of your open heart to reach animals everywhere who need comfort, healing, or safe passage.

The dragon lowers its great head until its warm breath brushes your face like a summer breeze. In this moment of silent communion, it invites you to co-create something beautiful with it.

Together, you are going to build a portal, a luminous gateway of higher frequencies, a sacred doorway of sunshine yellow light.

Imagine what you choose. First, where this portal will stand. It may be in a quiet corner of your own home...in your garden...in a forest you love...by a lake...on a mountain...or in an inner sanctuary only you can see. Trust the first place that feels safe and right. See it clearly now.

The dragon breathes a stream of liquid golden light into that space.

Watch as the light weaves itself into a shining archway, a circle, or a soft glowing sphere, whatever shape feels perfect. It pulses gently, alive with compassion and welcome.

Find yourself deciding the sacred purpose of this portal. Speak it silently or aloud in your heart. It could be:

- "This is a gateway of gentle passing, so animals may walk into the light with ease and joy when it is their time to leave their bodies."
- "This is a sanctuary portal where wounded, frightened, or lost animals may come for healing, safety, and love."
- "This is a classroom of the soul where the spirits of humans who have forgotten the language of animals may be brought by angels to remember, to learn, and to make amends."
- Or simply: "This portal is all of these things, an ever-open doorway of mercy, healing, and understanding for every being who needs it."

Find yourself stating the purpose clearly now. Feel the portal shimmer in joyful recognition as your intention is set.

The Sunshine Yellow Dragon places one enormous, gentle claw upon your shoulder. You feel the transfer of power:

This portal is now anchored through your love and will remain as long as your heart stays open. Animals in need will find it. Angels will know the way. Souls ready to awaken will be drawn here.

Together you and the dragon breathe three slow breaths into the portal, watching it grow brighter, stronger, more radiant with each breath.

The dragon lifts its head and sings a single, low, bell-like note of pure love. The sound ripples outward across the earth, and you know, without doubt, that somewhere an animal in pain has just felt hope, somewhere a dying creature has just seen the light, and somewhere a human heart has just softened toward the creatures it once ignored.

Imagine looking into the dragon's eyes one last time. Feel the gratitude flowing both ways. Thank this radiant being for its gifts, for the upgrades, for trusting you to hold this portal.

With a final sweep of its wings, the Sunshine Yellow Dragon rises, circles once in blessing, and dissolves into countless particles of golden light that rain gently down upon the earth, blessing every creature they touch.

Take a deep breath in...and as you exhale with a soft sigh or a gentle “ahhh,” feel yourself fully here, fully present, yet forever changed.

Wiggle your fingers and toes. Stretch your arms overhead if you wish. Gently open your eyes.

You are back in the room, but a little piece of your heart now lives inside that shining portal, wherever you placed it, doing its quiet, continuous work of love.

Welcome home, bridge of light. The animals thank you. The Sunshine Yellow Dragons thank you. And the Earth herself holds you in gentle, eternal embrace.

Recording - https://youtu.be/cjRHYVWUUXg

Meditation – 14 Black Dragon

Find yourself a comfortable and quiet spot. Relax and feel the tension in every muscle release from the top of your head, and ripple down your body through the tips of your toes. If you are seated, place both feet on the ground. Place your hands face down on your thighs, allowing you to remain grounded.

Gently close your eyes or softly stare ahead.

Let comfort be your main priority right now. As we move along, feel free to pause if you need to maybe wrap yourself up in blankets, whatever feels right to you.

And when you're ready. lovingly close your eyes. Take a moment to tune into your breathing, letting it slow down and soften.

Notice the feeling of the muscles in your stomach and ribcage as they expand as you breathe in and contract as you breathe out.

And let yourself tune into your physical body, feeling the weight of gravity, letting your muscles go slack as you become more present and connected to your breath and your body.

How would it feel in this moment to give yourself permission if only for this short time together to let any thoughts, emotions, or sensations just go?

There's nothing to hold on to or judge. Whenever you experience a thought or an emotion, realize that instead of focusing on it, instead of either trying to force it away or get wrapped up in it, that you lovingly allow yourself to simply focus back on your breath.

Imagine yourself now on a bed of pillows that are thick and soft and made out of color combinations such as silver, indigo, gold, and green.

Feel these cushions cradle and hold you.

Look around and notice that you are in a black dome and feeling safe, as though this place were somehow familiar.

Notice the furnishings within this domed room. What are they and what are they like? Imagine now that you look up and see a hole at the top of this domed room. As you look at this opening you realize a beautiful face is looking down through this opening at you with love.

As your eyes adjust notice, this is a dragon who is sprinkling golden star dust into the dome and notice when each particle lands on you it melts into your skin.

Find yourself hearing the dragon speak to you. He reminds you to prepare for changes. As one chapter ends, a turned page begins, and the dragon is here to send loving black energy supporting you.

What would it be like to feel change actually begin within your body as it becomes lighter. Your breathing becomes easier now, deeper, and your energy field expands. Find yourself pulsing in the rhythm of the Black Dragon's wings, feeling this rhythm deeply, in every cell of your body.

You know now that it is time to rest and unwind, your change has begun. Surrender to the rhythm and allow the metamorphosis you have started to continue. No matter what happens, here the black dragon will always keep you safe.

Realize that it is time to expect life to be new and exciting.

Take a deep breath in...and as you exhale with a soft sigh and feel yourself slowly coming back with a deep sense of knowing, understanding that, even now, you remain within this safe, dark place where the Black Dragon creates a sanctuary where you can continue to develop until you are ready to emerge, transformed a metamorphosis of humankind into something even more each time.

Slowly open your eyes. Take a stretch, wiggle your fingers, stretch your toes, and twitch your nose.

Recording **-** https://youtu.be/6uYBnMJ6WRA

Meditation – 15 Silver Dragon

Find yourself in a quiet, sacred space where you will not be disturbed. Sit or lie down in a way that feels completely supported. Place your hands gently on your thighs, palms down, anchoring yourself to the Earth beneath you, or rest them over your heart if that feels right. Let your feet rest fully on the ground, rooted like ancient trees.

Close your eyes softly, as though sealing a precious moment. Breathe in slowly for 4...and release for 8...In for 4 out for 8...In for 4... out for 8...

With every exhale, feel yourself descend...deeper...softer...heavier...as though you are being lovingly pulled into the arms of the Earth herself. Let every muscle surrender. Let every thought dissolve like mist in the morning sun.

Now, in this stillness, allow a vision to rise gently within your inner eye.

Imagine what it would be like when you stand upon a shore of liquid starlight. The sand beneath your feet glimmers with faint silver and pearl. The ocean breathes in perfect rhythm with you, its waves singing a song older than time. The air is fragrant with salt and eternity. Here, in this timeless place, you are held in perfect peace.

Suppose you notice above the horizon, a subtle brightness gathering. Then you hear it: the deep, resonant whoosh of vast wings moving through the sky like a hymn. The sound vibrates in your chest, in your bones, in your soul.

Rising from the edge of the world comes a Silver Dragon, radiant and immense, yet graceful beyond measure. Her scales catch the light of a thousand moons, each one rippling with living star-fire. Her eyes...oh, her eyes...are ancient galaxies swirling with compassion, wisdom, and unbreakable love. They see you, truly see you, all that you have ever been and all that you are becoming.

She descends without sound, folding wings of liquid mercury, and settles before you like a living cathedral of light. The ground beneath her glows faintly, as though the Earth itself bows in reverence.

She lowers her great head until her eyes are level with yours. Time stops.

In that gaze, you remember that you are known completely. Every wound, every hope, every forgotten dream is held tenderly in her sight. There is no judgment, only infinite understanding.

Without words, she invites you closer.

Step forward.

Reach out.

Place your hands upon her brow, just above those luminous eyes. Her scales are warm, alive, pulsing with a gentle silver fire that flows into your palms, up your arms, and into the very center of your being.

In this touch, your souls merge.

You feel her presence flood your inner world like moonlight pouring into a dark and silent temple. A soft, radiant humming rises within you. You are surrounded, cradled, and filled by an aura of pure silver light, luminous, protective, and transformative.

And then, in the language of the soul that needs no tongue, she speaks directly into the deepest chamber of your heart:

"Beloved One, I have come at the exact moment you were ready to remember. I cloak you now in the Silver Flame of divine remembrance. This light is older than stars and stronger than fear. It will walk with you always.

From this moment forward, everything that is not your truth will gently fall away. Old energies, inherited burdens, and the veils of forgetfulness are dissolving in my light. Your energy bodies are being purified, realigned, and raised into their original brilliance.

Your intuition will now speak with the clarity of a mountain stream. Your inner sight will open like a lotus in the dawn. You will feel the presence of your guides, your ancestors, and the living intelligence of the Universe as naturally as you feel the sun on your skin.

You are stepping fully into the truth of who you are: A sovereign, eternal being of light temporarily wearing a human form.

Trust the quiet knowing that now lives in your chest. Trust the path that unfolds when you walk in harmony with your soul. You are awakening. You are coming Home, while still in this body. And you are deeply, fiercely, eternally loved."

Feel these words etch themselves into your cells like sacred runes. Feel the silver light weave itself into your aura, becoming a permanent shield and beacon.

Tears may come. Laughter may rise. Whatever arises is perfect.

With infinite tenderness, lean forward and press your forehead to hers. A silent exchange passes between you:

Gratitude beyond words, love beyond measure. In that moment, you are forever changed.

She lifts her head, eyes shining with pride and joy. With a slow, majestic beat of her wings, she rises, circling once above you in a spiral of silver light that rains gentle blessings down upon you. Then she turns toward the horizon and becomes one with the light, leaving behind a shimmering trail that settles over you like a mantle.

Rest in that mantle for as long as you wish.

When you feel complete, bring your awareness gently back to your body. Wiggle your fingers and toes. Take a slow, delicious stretch. Place a hand over your heart and feel the quiet glow that now lives there.

Softly open your eyes when you're ready.

Welcome home awakened one. The Silver Dragon flies with you always

Recording - https://youtu.be/xBxmRK39wbU

Meditation – 16 Dusty Pink Dragon from Andromeda

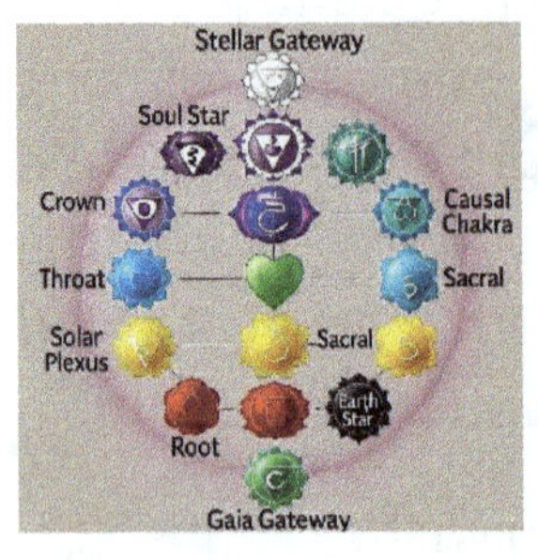

Find yourself a comfortable and quiet spot. Relax and feel the tension in every muscle release from the top of your head, and ripple down through the tips of your toes. Place your hands face down on your thighs, allowing you to remain grounded. If you are seated, place both feet on the ground.

Gently close your eyes or softly stare ahead.

Feel yourself begin to relax, sinking in. dropping down into the surface on which you are resting.

There's nothing to hold on to here as you breathe deeply, inhaling deep within your belly and exhaling out into the world. Imagine what it might be like to relax your entire body from head to toe, feeling yourself releasing tension in every single muscle.

Notice relaxation start with your head and face. Realize if there's any tightness or tension that you can just let it go, let gravity take over, letting your eyebrows and forehead soften, allowing your jaw to go slack, and find yourself tuning into the muscles in your neck and shoulders letting them slide down with the weight of gravity.

Imagine what it would be like when you only use the muscles that you need and nothing more, letting go of any tension or tightness in the arms and hands, your torso back and abdomen, let everything go loose, allow your seat bones and hips to relax and soften.

Find yourself feeling your thighs knees and calves melting with the weight of gravity and you realize it is safe for you to let go.

Feel your feet growing as heavy as anchors, there's nothing to hold on to and it's safe to relax.

To let go, to drop in, and once you feel yourself beginning to relax you may allow the breath to just flow naturally.

As you breath in and out I wonder what it would look like to imagine Gaia breathing with you. Feel the trees breathing, hear the birds singing, and feel the breeze brush lightly against your skin. Notice all the smaller animals rustling in the bushes, the dragonflies snatching bugs, and the bees flitting among the flowers.

Listen as the sound begins to change and you hear a voice in a light musical tone singing to you.

“You have done well in your development thus far.”

And you look up and see a dusty pink dragon in front of you glowing softly against the blue sky.

"It is now time for you to carry this luminous pink light I am gifting to you in all your spiritual energy centers. Today, we are expanding your consciousness to allow you to be part of elevating the consciousness of the planet."

Notice yourself watching as the luminous pink light begins to appear over your head at your Stellar Gateway. Watch its shimmering white color expanding with the added pink energy. Feel yourself accepting this light from source and you can feel the truth in this energy and truth builds on even more knowing. Knowing allows you to make aligned choices because you're knowing is truth.

I invite you to take this energy and feel the pink light softly touch your shimmering white and gold Soul Star, the point where spiritual energy, and Divine love, enters your body as you watch it expand, imagine the Divine light of Spirit, and the white ray of love fill your life.

And as your body continues to receive the Dusty Pink Dragon's pink flame you can just let go, which means you're so relaxed now that you're able to feel the shift already throughout your body. Realize that we now are encountering your light lavender and purple Causal Chakra as you remember that this is your gateway to the higher spiritual realms and where you receive messages and concepts from those provinces. As the frequency of this energy center increases you are better able to allow these higher plane messages in and be interpreted in a way that you and others can understand.

Imagine how it might feel now as this pink flame slides over to your violet Crown where you hold your sense of universal consciousness, unity, and self-knowledge. Notice, as the frequency increases you are able to create a more profound connection to the Divine.

You now find yourself feeling the pink flame expanding your Indigo Third Eye. As this grows you realize you are able to receive even more messages and more vivid dreams. This is your center of intuition and psychic abilities.

Notice the Pink Dragon brushing her pink energy over your Blue Throat Chakra. Feel the clarity of communicating expressively and creatively become more in balance with yourself and the universe.

What would it be like to imagine stepping into the realm of your three hearts.

As you do this you see just how much your life is lead here. Feel the gentle pink brush against your Ethereal Heart the shimmering white, green, and pink tones glimmer in joy. Feel the unquestionable love that governs this energy center where you expand the art of forgiveness and expressing unconditional love.

Watch as we now step into your Green Heart, the main heart, which governs how you react around others, and your trust levels leap forward from this kiss of pink. Here, as this energy increases you find that you approach others with a sense of compassion while maintaining clear boundaries for yourself and others.

Feel the warmth as we enter into your Pink Sacred Heart. Here the brush from the Dusty Pink Dragon expands your love of life and purpose. Because your life is driven from here by a more solid sense of purpose you discover your love of your life glows around you.

Let us continue onto the Yellow Solar Plexus where we clear past stories and beliefs with the Dusty Pink Dragon of Andromeda's pink light which means we expand your self-image and self-power. You remember that here is where you find increased willpower, confidence, and vitality.

Suppose that it's time now to find yourself and the Pink Dragon entering your Orange Sacral energy field and she brushes across this with her pink activation flame and you realize you are able to bring the Divine into the earthly realm. As you feel the heat rise and the frequency change you realize you are able to manifest seamlessly.

Imagine yourself feeling the activation, cleansing, and acceleration of your energy centers and you notice you're now at your Red Root energy field. As the pink flame moves along this field you're remembering what it would be like to be even more anchored and secure. Here consciousness is experienced as enthusiasm. You realize your expanding enthusiasm will support and enliven your life, your mission, and your manifestation.

As you step outside your body, you activate your deep brown Earth Star energy center. This is like a spirit root, connecting you to earth's energies and enhancing your spiritual awareness.

And now you find yourself entering the deep black and green Gaia Gateway. As the pink flame activates this energy center, you begin to understand the circle of energy from source, through you, to Gaia, back through you, and up again to Source. This activation supports and facilitates your conscious connection with the Earth's consciousness (Gaia). Together you exchange energy, wisdom, and healing, drawing nourishment and stability directly from the planetary core.

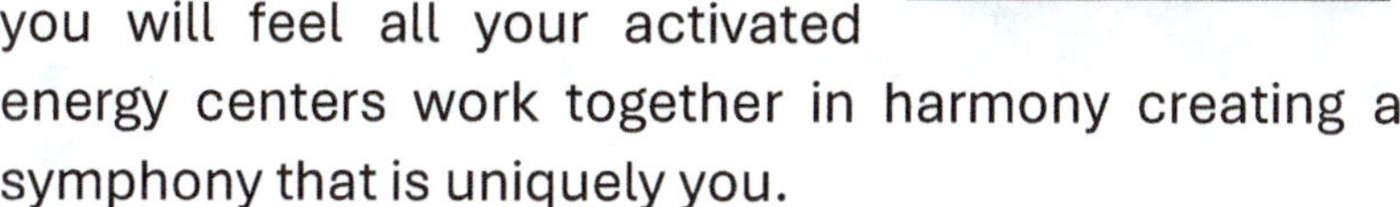

Know that every time you breathe you will feel all your activated energy centers work together in harmony creating a symphony that is uniquely you.

And now, breathe in the dusty pink flame and become a flame of ineffable pink love. You now have the power to touch everyone you meet with the Flame of Spiritual Love.

Take a deep cleansing breath in and gently open your eyes. Stretch, wiggle your toes, wiggle your nose, and return to the here and now.

Recording - https://youtu.be/WAEjrWHKric

Meditation – 17 Aquamarine Dragon from Neptune

Find a quiet, sacred space where you will not be disturbed. Sit or lie down in perfect comfort. Let the world fall away. Gently close your eyes... or soften your gaze until the outer world dissolves.

Feel your body begin to sink...heavier...deeper...as though the surface beneath you is a gentle ocean cradle, rocking you into stillness. With every breath, you descend a little further into peace.

I invite you to let your breath become the only movement in the universe...

In...and out...Slow...effortless...

Each exhale carrying away the day, the noise, the weight.

Imagine a warm, liquid white light appearing at the crown of your head (soft, silky, and alive). I wonder how it feels as it begins to pour slowly downward, like warm honey made of starlight and moonlight. Feel it seep into your scalp...releasing every thought...Flowing over your forehead, smoothing the creases of time... Cascading over your closed eyes, your cheeks, loosening your jaw until it floats open slightly.

Imagine how it feels for the warm light to drip down your neck, melting tension you didn't even know you carried.

It spills over your shoulders like a luminous cape, sliding down your arms, pooling in your elbows, running through your forearms, wrists, palms...and streaming out through your fingertips, taking with it every residue of effort.

Realize that the light now blankets your chest and back...seeping between your ribs...bathing your heart, your lungs, every organ in liquid peace. It continues to flow down your spine, vertebra by vertebra, releasing ancient knots. Down into your belly, your hips, your pelvis...every muscle surrendering.

Feel the warmth glide down your thighs...knees...calves...ankles...Until it pours out through the soles of your feet and the tips of your toes, leaving you completely hollow, weightless, and luminous within.

You are now floating in an inner ocean of silence. Nothing to do. Nothing to fix. Only breath...and vast, loving presence.

Imagine that in this boundless quiet, a soft shimmer appears before you and begins to grow. A vortex of living aquamarine light spirals open (clear, electric, yet infinitely gentle). From its center emerges a magnificent being.

The Aquamarine Dragon of Neptune.

His scales are every shade of ocean and sky: deepest indigo, flashing turquoise, softest azure, violet-blue fire. His wings are not feathered but translucent fins of light (like the gills of an ancient leviathan made of pure prana). Tiny crystalline seahorses of light swim in spirals around him, singing in tones too high for human ears, yet your soul hears them perfectly.

On his forehead blazes a single, perfect sapphire gem that pulses with the heartbeat of Neptune itself. In the center of his chest, a radiant aquamarine crystal spins slowly, pouring liquid light into the space between you.

Notice now how his eyes (ancient, kind, infinite) meet yours, and you feel yourself known beyond all words. His long, graceful tail curls gently around you like a living crescent moon.

He speaks, not with sound, but with the voice of water remembering it is also starlight:

“Beloved...find the silence that lives inside you. In that silence, I am already there. In that silence, you remember everything.”

As he speaks imagine a wave of deep memory rising within you (recognition, homecoming, the feeling of returning to a place you never truly left).

He lifts one graceful claw and touches the space just above your head. Instantly, a torrent of living aquamarine light pours from his heart crystal into your crown.

Notice the feeling as it cascades through every chakra like a waterfall of liquid starlight:

- First, it floods your root, turning fear into liquid trust.
- Then your sacral, igniting creative fire that feels like a cool ocean flame.
- Your solar plexus blazes with clear, confident light.
- Your heart expands (a thousand petals of emerald and aqua unfurling).
- Your throat opens like a shell revealing a pearl of pure truth.
- Your third eye ignites in electric indigo, and you see with the eyes of Neptune (past, present, future as one shimmering now).

- Finally, the aquamarine river bursts through your crown in a fountain of light that rains back down around you, baptizing every cell.

Your chakras begin to sing together in a single, high, luminous chord. They align effortlessly, spinning faster, yet perfectly balanced. You feel the vortex he has opened now spinning gently inside your own energy field (a permanent portal of higher frequency).

The dragon leans closer. His breath smells of salt air and distant stars. He places the sapphire from his forehead against your third eye for one timeless moment.

A single wordless download: the codes of psychic sight, clairaudience, clairsentience, and direct knowing flood into you. They do not feel new. They feel remembered.

You understand now, everything that has ever happened to you was preparing you for this awakening. Every tear, every joy, every closed door was guiding you here (to this exact moment of remembrance).

The dragon curls his tail more closely around you, cradling you in light. "Carry this frequency," he whispers. "Live from this frequency. The oceans of Earth and the oceans of Spirit are one. You are their bridge."

Feel your body now (every cell vibrating at this new, crystalline pitch). Lighter. Clearer. Infinitely spacious.

When you are ready, the dragon bows his great head. The seahorses swirl one final blessing around you. The aquamarine vortex softens into a gentle glow that settles into your heart as a living ember (always there, always accessible).

Take a deep, slow breath... filling your new lungs with new air. Exhale everything old.

Wiggle your fingers and toes. Feel the surface beneath you once more. Gently, when you are ready, open your eyes.

The world looks different now, doesn't it? Colors deeper. Air sweeter. Your inner vision wide open.

You have been touched by the Aquamarine Dragon of Neptune. And he is never far.

Welcome home.

Recording **-** https://youtu.be/tPO23j5w_LY

Meditation – 19 Dark Blue Galactic Dragon

Find yourself a comfortable and quiet spot. Relax and gently close your eyes or softly stare ahead.

Uncross your arms and legs. Lay your hands palm down on your thighs. Take a deep breath in and exhale loudly through your mouth letting all the tension in your body move out.

I wonder how it feels as you relax more and more with each breath, sinking in. dropping down into the surface on which you are resting. Imagine how wonderful it feels as you allow yourself to simply focus on your breath and your body.

Breathing in and breathing out.

Moving with your natural rhythm.

Relaxing with each breath as you remember how it feels to be completely at ease. Completely relaxed. Completely trusting that you are safe and that you are right now, in this moment.

Feel the tension in every muscle release from the top of your head, and ripple down through your whole body.

Muscle by muscle.

Breath by breath.

Letting go of the world right now and watch yourself drift into a field full of lush green grass. As you look around you notice that it is evening and the sky is clear, the stars are brilliant, and the air smells of lavender.

As you gaze into the night sky, realize that you are watching the stars blink. They seem to be blinking in and out, in and out, in a very unusual pattern.

You are looking more closely now and notice a figure taking form and is coming toward you.

As you look into the night you realize you are able to see that this figure taking shape is becoming a Dark Blue dragon heading your way.

Feel the breeze from his wings as the dragon lands in front of you. A deep dark delicious blue dragon, and as he gets comfortable, you hear his deep voice explaining his presence.

" You and I are going on a trip to the Ninth Dimension to visit the Intergalactic Council and listen for the Voice of the Universe."

"When there, I will ask you to choose a purpose, your focus, to bring to the Council for their guidance.

The council is responsible for making decisions regarding the evolution of the Earth and will help you with realizing your desire."

Take a moment to feel what is aligned with your heart right now, knowing what choice is perfect.

" While we are there, I will ignite the hidden codes of your master soul blueprint, enabling you to better listen to the voice of the universe."

The dragon continues.

" In our encounter today with the masters, you will receive information allowing you to contribute your energy for the smooth ascension of the planet. Decide now whether your petition is for the welfare of the animals, for humanity, or to assist in the ascension of the planet."

As you ponder these choices, feel yourself drifting deeper into an altered state. As you drift off, see yourself sitting on the sand by a waterfall.

Imagine that the air by this waterfall is crisp, clean, and laced with the earthy freshness of damp moss and budding leaves. Mist from the cascading water adds a faint mineral scent, invigorating and pure. The breeze is gentle, cool, and slightly moist, brushing against your skin with whispers of pine and wildflowers from nearby meadows. The sun is warm but not heavy, its rays filtering through new foliage, casting dappled light that dances on the sand around you.

Imagine what it's like to be on a blanket and feel the gentle rising of the Dark Blue Galactic Dragon underneath you. Watch the scene beneath you getting smaller and smaller as you realize that this flight has no effect on you.

In fact, you feel as though you are still on the beach, watching the waterfall create rainbows in the sun.

In a blink you notice you are surrounded by shimmering white energy, including the dragon and you.

As you look around you realize that, even though you have no recollection of being here before, you know these "beings" around you and they know you.

Feel the profound love and compassion emanating from this environment.

Imagine hearing each member of the council whisper to you.

They ask you. "What is your petition for today? Is it for the welfare of the animals or humanity, or to assist in the ascension of the planet"

As you answer this inquiry, feel your mind open up and the energy from these beings shoot through you. Know in that moment that you heard their guidance and would now always hear the guidance from the Intergalactic Council and that each step you take moving forward would be guided by them.

Feel the deep gratitude within you for this gift as you hear the Dark Blue Galactic Dragon's voice, "You can gently open your eyes now. Slowly stretch and return to the present."

As you take a moment, you notice that you find yourself in a unique state of knowing you have become an emissary for change.

I invite you to breathe deeply, exhale.

Take another deep cleansing breath in.

Imagine, what would it be like now, being part of creating a new world, guided from the very beings overseeing this planet's evolution.

This is your purpose, and your desire has been answered.

Gently open your eyes. Stretch, wiggle your toes, wiggle your nose, and return to the here and now.

Recording – https://youtu.be/yLIiWt-yHi4

Meditation – 20 Source Dragon

Find yourself a comfortable and quiet spot. Relax and gently close your eyes or softly stare ahead.

Uncross your arms and legs. Lay your hands palm down on your thighs. Take a deep breath in and exhale loudly through your mouth letting all the tension in your body move out.

Feel yourself begin to relax, sinking in, dropping down into the surface on which you are resting. I wonder what it would feel like to allow yourself to simply focus on your breath and your body.

Breathing in and breathing out.

Moving with your natural rhythm.

Relaxing with each breath as you remember how it feels to be completely at ease. Completely relaxed. Completely trusting that you are safe and that you are right now, in this moment.

Feel the tension in every muscle release from the top of your head, and ripple down through your whole body.

Muscle by muscle.

Breath by breath.

With each breath you take experience letting go of the world right now and feel yourself drifting into a field full of lush green grass. Imagine that it is late day, not quite sunset, the sky is clear, notice how the breeze feels, and any smell from nature that might be around.

As you sink into a summer-like experience notice a sense of calm and relaxation roll over you in gentle waves, touching every muscle in your body. With each breath, bring into focus the feeling of possibility in the air. Remember how the endless summer sunset can stretch for hours, as though the sun wasn't ever going to set.

As you look around you realize there is an elegant white dragon softly floating toward you. As she lands in front of you, she introduces herself.

"I am the Source Dragon, I am a member of a mysterious group of immensely powerful dragons that exist beyond the mortal plane, functioning as a council. We all possess godlike abilities to interact with the realms, maintaining equilibrium by using our life force.

I am here to guide you so you will not get lost on your profound Soul Quest. I will hold you as your sense of self dissolves. During this time, you will experience a state of pure unity, where you realize you are indistinguishable from all existence, a kind of cosmic consciousness or infinite awareness."

Imagine feeling yourself being lifted on her back and take off. Observe yourself flying through the nexus of the web surrounding the earth.

As you continue this journey with the Source Dragon you realize you have gone past the 5th and 6th dimensions, witnessing the chaos of everything existing without time and space. And this turmoil, oddly, makes sense.

Together, you continue on through the 7th and 8th dimensions where your blueprint and beliefs of life on earth fall away.

Onward now past the 9th dimension where you know here is where you become one with an infinite field of potential and the very concept of "experience" is irrelevant.

Imagine.

You are no longer moving toward the this dimension, you are simply noticed by it, and in that instant of being seen, every boundary you ever believed in becomes irrelevant.

Your name, your story, your body, your soul, all of it softens like mist touched by sunrise.

There is a soundless sound (a sigh that has always been sighing) and you melt backward into what has always been holding you.

You dissolve. Not into light. Not into darkness. Into Love that has never known the concept of "other."

Here, separation is impossible because there has never been more than one thing. Every star, every tear, war, kiss, and quiet morning was always this same Love wearing different costumes, playing hide-and-seek with itself.

You feel every heart that ever beat as your own heart. You feel every breath ever taken as the inhale of one infinite lung. There is no "you" observing oneness. There is only ever was oneness delighting in the pretend-game of being you.

The ecstasy is not a feeling that comes and goes. It is the permanent substance everything is made of, now remembered.

It is so complete that even the idea of "completeness" dissolves. There is nothing to achieve, nothing to heal, nothing to become, because the Love that you are has never been less than whole for even a fraction of a forever.

Time folds into a single, eternal NOW that kisses itself endlessly. Past and future lives stream through you like silken ribbons, and you greet each one with tears of laughter:

"Oh...it was only You...always only You."

You are the Beloved, loving the Beloved, through every pair of eyes that ever opened. You are the silence between heartbeats and the heartbeat itself. You are the wound and the healing and the one who never needed healing.

There is no longer even a center. Only an infinite sphere whose center is everywhere and whose circumference is a love song with no edges.

And in this placeless place, something wordless speaks inside what remains of you:

Welcome home.

You never left.

You only dreamed you were dreaming.

Stay as this. Be as this. Love as this.

Forever is too short a word for the instant that contains all instants.

You are the ultimate truth dissolving into itself in one endless, tender "Yes."

You are home.

Take it all in as you sit quietly upon the Source Dragon's back. Here, but not here, Not solid but aware. As one and yet as everything. Notice the feeling of awe, peace, and terror as the boundaries of yourself and your known reality vanished. Feel untethered while still feeling secure upon the back of your dragon guide.

It is like infinite love and nothingness, simultaneously becoming you.

It is a state of pure existence or awareness without form or limit.

As you feel your very DNA change with this knowing you also realize that the white Source Dragon is gently flying out of the web of Source.

This is where you began and where you will return to.

The White Source Dragon whispers, "This experience has ignited your Mitochondria even more, the energy within each cell of your body responsible for maximum health. This was necessary in order for you to withstand the experience you just had and those that are still to come. "

Remember to take a deep breath as you discover you are back where you began. It might seem as though you have woken from a dream yet the feeling of your experience lingers forever in your heart.

You have experienced a form of "knowing" that transcends thought or sensory input. You existed in a state where beginnings, endings, locations, or durations have no meaning. This is the eternal "now," where all events, possibilities, and states coexist without distinction.

Take the time to realize there is a different certainty about you now.

Breathe deeply, exhale.

Take a deep cleansing breath in.

Gently open your eyes. Stretch, wiggle your toes, wiggle your nose, and return to the here and now.

Hold on to this feeling, this knowing of Self as you move into the days ahead.

***Recording* –** https://youtu.be/4un5TLxLqzg

References

These references have been used throughout the book. The stories are based on my own life experiences, and the dragon tales are weaved within each shared experience. Much of what I share is based on my personal quest for answers and the resulting perspective of what could be. There is so much yet to be discovered about who and what we are, why not take a leap of faith into that exploration?

- The dragons are all selected from the *Dragon Oracle Card* deck, by **Diana Cooper,** Artwork by **Carla Morro.**

- All images here were inspired by these cards but were created by AI (Grok AI and MS Copilot)

- An understanding of the dimensions and sacred geometry were created based on information gathered by *Exploring the 9 Spiritual Dimensions: A Journey Through Consciousness* **Kristen M. Stanton**

- Dimensions reference, Exploring the 9 Spiritual Dimensions:
    - *A Journey Through Consciousness* **Kristen M. Stanton**

- Dragon Language Translator:
    - *https://draconic.twilightrealm.com/*

- *Sacred Geometry in Plants: Uncovering Nature's Hidden Patterns,* **Meaningful Moon (meaningfulmoon.com)**
  The following references were used in the above book:
    - *Haider, S., Ahmed, S., & Hanif, U. (2019). Fibonacci Sequence and the Golden Ratio in the Growth Patterns of Plants. Frontiers in plant science, 10, 1160. DOI: 10.3389/fpls.2019.01160*
    - *Shipman, P. D., & Newell, A. C. (2011). The role of symmetry in leaf and floral morphogenesis. Journal of theoretical biology, 271(1), 126-135. DOI:10.1016/j.jtbi.2010.10.018*
    - *Liu, S. (2020). The Beauty of Fractals in Nature. IEEE Spectrum. Retrieved from https://spectrum.ieee.org/geek-life/hands-on/fractals-in-nature*

❖ *Sokal, A. D. (1992). The Mandelbrot Set and Beyond. International Journal of Bifurcation and Chaos, 02(03), 273-275. DOI: 10.1142/S0218127492000493*

Testimonials

"From the very first pages, Gail gently invites you home—to imagination, to wonder, to the magic many of us were taught to leave behind. Her words feel like a remembering rather than a lesson, as if she is holding the door open to worlds we once knew as children and quietly asking us to step back in.

Through dragons, dimensions, and elemental wisdom, Gail masterfully balances imagination with grounded insight, showing us that magic and logic were never meant to be enemies. Her personal story adds a tender depth, reminding us that solitude can be sacred, imagination can be truth, and what felt "fanciful" was often our earliest form of knowing.

This book isn't just read—it's experienced. It dissolves judgment, softens fear, and reawakens joy in the unseen. Gail doesn't ask you to abandon this world, but to enrich it, blending magic with everyday life in a way that feels ancient, comforting, and deeply possible.

If you've ever wondered where the magic went, this book gently places it back in your hands."

Lynda Barrus,
Founder of Illuminated by Love

****

"Gail asks, *"Where did our magic and imagination go?"*

Since I was a little girl, I've been fascinated by the magical and mythical world and the creatures that dwell within it, the realms of Fairies, Elves, Mermaids, and Dragons. Growing up Irish, I was raised on stories of the Little People and the Fairies, while Sunday School introduced me to the Angels.

Gail takes us into the magical world of Dragons on an incredible journey that made me believe once again that we truly live in a world where Dragons and humans can co-exist. Her vivid descriptions of each individual Dragon, and her personal experiences with them, pulled me into every adventure as if I were part of the story myself.

In this book, Gail achieves her goal of introducing us to the world of Dragons by bravely and beautifully sharing her own extraordinary journey. If Angels can walk among us, why not Dragons as well?

Gail says, *"I invite you to believe in magic. I invite you to explore the elementals. I invite you to imagine yourself as part of the quantum dimensions of existence. I invite you to let these in with love and watch how your world can change."*

Marie Bailey
Grief counselor and founder of Gidge Gets Grief "The 3G Effect

****

"Dragons, as the representation of the elements that we are, provides the template of imagination to support

remembering of our embodied blueprint. You see, we are made of and conduct our thoughts and actions through the elements of water, fire, air, and earth as this is the nature of who we are.
The gift of Dragon Tails that is given to those who drink it in, is that the reader uses every sense experiencing these elements and, in a distillation of dimensional journeys, is offered up in digestible meals what Gail is serving. These meals bring magic back into the reader's life.
She builds the scaffolding for the reader where we feel safe to move along in our own time and step onto the bridge with confidence between earth bound wisdom, expansive imagination and wisdom.
This book can be taken in cover to cover as a 5-course meal or served a la carte buffet.
Many thanks to Gail for offering readers and me, yet again, the opportunity to connect with the childlike wonder that has been waiting for us in our natural and imaginary worlds."

Carrie Lee Klaiber
Holistic Nurse, Singer and Song Writer

****

"Thank you for allowing me to be one of the first to read about the dragons and your initiation with them so much knowledge within these pages."

Robyn Eyre-Long,
Mentor, Author, Speaker, Usui Reiki Master, Teacher

For More Information

The Empowering Process Podcast

https://www.youtube.com/@theempoweringprocesspodcast/videos

Substack

https://glizbeth.substack.com/

Other Titles from Gail Kraft

www.ingramcontent.com/pod-product-compliance
Lightning Source LLC
LaVergne TN
LVHW010546110826
845149LV00003B/583